Contents

1. Sam Pig's Trousers   7
2. Sam Pig and the Wind   19
3. Sam Pig and the Dragon   34
4. Sam Pig and the Cuckoo Clock   52
5. Sam Pig and the Irishmen   71
6. The Leprechaun   85
7. The Theatre   101
8. The Flower Show   114
9. The Snow Goose   129
10. The Christmas Box   144

Sam Pig's Trousers

Sam Pig was always hard on his trousers. He tore them on the brambles and hooked them in the gorse bushes. He lost little pieces of them in the hawthorns, and he left shreds among the spiky thistles. He rubbed them threadbare with sliding down the rocks of the high pastures, and he wore them into holes when he scrambled through hedges. One always knew where Sam Pig had been by the fragments of check trousers which clung to thorn and crooked twig. The birds were very glad, and they took bits to make their nests. The rooks had little snippets like gay pennons dangling from their rookery in the elms, and the chaffinches and yellow-hammers mixed the threads with sheep's wool to line their beds. It seemed as if Sam Pig would provide material for everybody's home in the trees and hedgerows, but trousers won't last for ever, and Sam's were nearly done.

Sister Ann patched the seats and put pieces into the front. She stitched panels in the two sides, and then she patched and repatched the patches until there was none of the original trousers left. They were a conglomeration of stripes and plaids and spotted scraps, all herring-boned and cross-stitched with green thread.

'Sam's trousers are like a patchwork quilt,' remarked Tom, when Ann held up the queer little garments one evening after she had mended them.

'Pied and speckled like a magpie,' said Bill.

Sam Pig leaned out of the truckle bed where he lay wrapped in a blanket, waiting for Ann to finish the mending. They were the only trousers the little pig possessed, and he had to go to bed early on mending nights.

'I like them patched,' said he indignantly. 'Don't mock at them. I love my old trousers and their nice patches. It's always a surprise when Ann finishes them. Look now! There's a green patch on top of a black patch, on top of a yellow patch, on top of a blue one. And there's lots of pockets hidden among the patches, spaces where I can keep things. When Ann's stitches burst I stuff things in between.'

'Yes,' frowned Ann, 'I've already taken out a ladybird, and a piece of honey-comb, and some bees, and a frog that was leaping up and down, and a stag-beetle that was fighting, not to mention sundry pebbles and oak-apples and snail shells! No wonder you look a clumsy shape with all those things hidden in your patches, Sam! All corners and lumps, you are!'

Sam curled himself under the blanket and laughed till he made the bed shake. She hadn't found the most important thing of all, something that was hidden under the largest patch! If she did — !

Just then Ann gave a shrill cry and dropped the trousers.

'Oh! They've bitten me! Your trousers bit my finger!' she exclaimed, and she put her hand in her mouth and sucked it.

'Trousers can't bite,' said Tom, but Sam dived deeper under the blanket, and laughed all the more.

'What is it, Sam?' asked Tom sternly. 'Confess! What is hidden there in your trousers?'

There was no answer, but from the patch came a pair of ears, and two bright eyes. A white mouse poked out its little head. It stared at Ann, it peeped at Sam, and then it bolted down the table leg and into a hole in the floor.

'Now you've lost her! You've lost Jemima!' said Sam crossly, coming up from the blankets. 'She was my pet mouse, and you've lost her. She was a most endearing creature. I kept her in that patch and fed her on crumbs. Is her family safe?'

'Family?' cried Ann, shrilly.

'Family?' echoed Bill and Tom.

'Yes. She has four children. They all live in the patch. They have a nest there. I helped Jemima to make it. I'm the godfather to the children. They know me very well.'

Ann hurriedly unpicked the stitches and brought out a small round nest with four pink mice inside it.

'There they are! Aren't they charming creatures?' cried Sam. 'But they will be lonely without their mother. You must put them by the hole in the floor, Ann, and Jemima will come for them. She'll miss her warm home in my trousers, and the food I give her.'

Ann carried the nest and placed it close to the hole. In a minute the mother appeared and enticed her brood away.

'Good-bye, Sam,' she squealed in a shrill voice, thin as a grasshopper's chirp. 'Good-bye Sam, and thank you for your hospitality. We are going to travel. It is time my children saw something of the world.'

'Good-bye,' called Sam, leaning out of bed. 'I shall miss you terribly, but we may meet again some day. The world is small.'

'Hm!' sniffed Ann Pig. 'The world may be small, but surely there is room in it for a family of white mice without their coming to live in a patch in your trousers, Sam.'

She threaded her needle and took up a bodkin and cleared away all the odds and ends the mice had left, their pots and frying-pan and toasting fork. She tossed the bits of cheese in the fire and frowned as she brought out a bacon rind.

'Bacon in the house of the four pigs is an insult,' said she sternly.

'It came from the grocer's shop, Ann. Really it did! Jemima's husband brought it for the family,' protested Sam.

'Then it's quite time you had a new pair of trousers, Sam. Jemima's husband bringing bacon rinds! I won't have it! These mice are the last straw!' cried Ann, and she banged the trousers and shook them and threw them back to Sam.

'Yes,' agreed Bill. 'It is time you had new breeks. We can't have a menagerie in our house. You'll keep ants and antelopes hidden in your patches, Sam, if you go on like this.'

'Bears and bisons,' said Tom, shaking his head at Sam.

'Crocodiles and cassowaries,' whispered Sam, quivering with laughter.

'It's no laughing matter. Trousers don't grow on gooseberry bushes.'

'I don't want a new pair,' pouted Sam. 'I know

this pair, and they are very comfortable. I know every stitch and cranny, and every ridge and crease and crumple.' He pulled the trousers on and shook himself.

'These will soon be quite worn out. One more tear and they will be done,' said Ann. 'We must get another pair, and where the stuff is to come from in these hard times I don't know. You'd better go collecting, all of you.'

'Collecting what? Trousers? From the scarecrows?' asked Sam.

'No. Sheep's wool. Get it off the hedges and bushes and fences. Everywhere you go you must gather the wool left by the sheep when they scramble through gaps and rub their backs on posts. Then I'll dye the wool and spin it, and make a new pair for you.'

Each day the pigs gathered sheep's wool. They picked it off the wild rose-trees, where it was twisted among the thorns. They got it from low fences under which the sheep had squeezed, and from the rough trunks of hawthorns and oaks where they had rubbed their backs. Sam found a fine bunch of fleecy wool where the flock had pushed under the crooked boughs of an ancient tree to sleep in the hollow beneath. It was surprising what a quantity of wool there was lying about in the country lanes, and each day they brought back their small sacks filled to the brim.

Ann washed the little fleeces and hung them up to dry. The wool was white as snow when she had finished dipping it in the stream. She tied it to a stout stick and swung it in the sunshine till it was dry and light as a feather.

Bill filled a bowl with lichens and mosses and pieces of bark, and Ann dyed the wool.

'What colour will it be?' asked Sam anxiously peering at it. 'I don't want brown or grey or anything dull.'

'It looks like drab,' confessed Ann.

'Oh dear! What a dingy shade!' sighed Sam. 'I don't want miserable gloomy trousers, or I shall be a gloomy little pig.'

'I'm afraid they *are* going to be sad trousers, Sam,' said Ann, stirring them with a stick. 'I'm sorry, but this is the colour, and there's one good thing, it is the colour of dirt.'

'Gloomy and black as a pitchy night in winter,' said Sam.

So off he went to the woods. He picked some crimson briony berries, and scarlet rose-hips, and bright red toadstools. He brought them back and dropped them into the dye.

'Ann! Ann! Come and look,' he called, and he held up the fleece on the end of the stirring stick.

'Oh Sam! Bright red! A glorious colour,' cried Ann.

'Like a sunset,' exclaimed Tom, admiringly.

'Like a house on fire,' said Bill.

Out rushed Sam again, for blueberries and blue geranium, and borage. He dipped another wisp of sheep's wool into the juices and brought it out blue as a wood in bluebell time.

They dried the wool, and Ann fastened it to her little spinning-wheel. She spun a length of red yarn and then a length of blue. Then she knitted a new pair of trousers, in blue and red checks, bright and bold, with plenty of real pockets.

When Sam Pig walked out in his new trousers all the animals and birds came to admire him. Even the Fox stopped to stare at Sam.

'As red as my brush,' he muttered, and the Hedgehog said, 'As pretty a pair of trousers as ever I seed in all my prickly life.'

When Sam met the white mouse and her family they refused to visit his new pockets.

'We like something quieter,' whispered the mouse. 'You are too dazzling for us nowadays, Sam.

Besides, we have found a lodging in an old boot. It
suits us better.'

'As you will, Jemima,' shrugged Sam. He saun-
tered off to show himself to acquaintances in the
fields, to visit his old haunts in wood and lane.

Soon his trousers lost their brightness, as they took
on the hues of the woodland. They were striped

green from the beech trunks, smeared with the juices of blackberry and spindle, patched by the brown earth herself. The sun faded them, the rain shrunk them, and the colours were softened by the moist airs.

'I declare! There is no difference in Sam's trousers,' Ann remarked one day. 'These might be the old check trousers; they are marked and stained in just the same way. I haven't patched them yet, but I can see a hole.'

'Yes,' said Sam, slyly, and he brought a dormouse from his pocket. 'Here is a little friend who lives with me, and he's waiting for a patch to make his winter sleeping-quarters, Ann.'

'Get along with you,' cried Ann, and she chased him out with a besom. But her eyes were twinkling as she watched her young brother dance down the garden path with his dormouse perched on his arm.

Sam Pig and the Wind

It was washing day and Ann Pig decided that it was time Sam's trousers were put in the washtub. They were new trousers, you will remember, made of sheep's wool, dyed red and blue in large checks, but they were dirty, for Sam had fallen into a pool of mud and stuck there till he was rescued.

So Ann scrubbed and rubbed them and hung them up to dry on the clothes-line in the crab-apple orchard, where they fluttered among pyjamas and handkerchiefs and the rest of the family wash.

Sam Pig stood near watching them, for he was afraid the Fox might steal them if he got the chance. It was a warm day, and Sam enjoyed having his little legs free.

'I'll stand on guard,' said he, 'then nobody can take my trousers for their nests or anything.'

The pair of trousers bobbed and danced on the clothes-line as if somebody were shaking them. It was the wind, which was blowing strongly. It came out of the clouds with a sudden swoop, and it puffed them and it huffed them, and it stuffed them with air. They really seemed to have a pair of invisible fat legs inside them as they swung to and fro and jigged and turned somersaults over the line.

The wind must have taken a fancy to those trousers for it gave a great tug and the wooden clothes-pegs fell to the ground. Sam Pig stooped to pick up his trousers, but they leapt away out of his grasp, and across the orchard. Sam sprang after them in a hurry. They frisked over the wall, struggled among the rough stones, and disappeared. Sam was sure they would be lying on the other side, and he climbed slowly and carefully to the top. Alas! The little trousers were already running swiftly across the meadow, trundling along the ground as if a pair of stout legs were inside them. Sam jumped down and ran after them at full speed. He nearly reached them, for the wind dropped and the little trousers flapped and fell empty to the ground. Just as Sam's arm was outstretched to grab them the wind swept down with a howl and caught them up again. It whirled them higher and higher, and tossed them into a tree.

'Whoo-oo-oo,' whistled the wind, as it shook them and left them. There they dangled, caught in a branch, like a dejected ninny. Sam Pig was not daunted. He began to climb that tree. He was part way up, clasping the slippery trunk, panting as he looked for a foothold, when the trousers disentangled themselves and fell to the earth.

'Hurrah!' cried Sam, and he slithered down to safety. 'Hurrah! Now I can get them.'

No! The wind swept down upon them. They rose on their little balloon legs and danced away. The wind blew stronger, and the trousers took leaps in the air like an acrobat. They turned head over heels; they danced on one leg and then on the other, like a sailor doing the hornpipe. Never were such dancing trousers seen as those windy wind-bags!

'Give me back my trousers, O wind,' called Sam Pig, and the wind laughed 'Who-o-o-o. Who-o-o,' and shrieked, 'Noo-oo-oo,' in such a shrill high voice that Sam shivered with the icy coldness of it.

The trousers jigged along the meadows and into the woods, with Sam running breathlessly after them. He tripped over brambles and caught his feet in rabbit holes and tumbled over tree trunks, but the trousers, wide-legged and active, leapt over the briars, and escaped the thorns as the wind tugged them away. When the wind paused a moment to take a deep breath Sam Pig got near, but he was never in time to catch the runaways. Sometimes they lay down for a rest, but as Sam crept up, stepping softly lest the

wind should hear, they sprang to their invisible feet
and scampered away.

'What's the matter, Sam?' asked the grey donkey
when Sam ran past with his arms outstretched and
his ears laid flat. 'Why are you running so fast?'

'My trousers! My trousers!' panted Sam. 'The
wind's got them, and it's blowing them away.'

'My goodness! It will blow them across the world,
Sam. You'll never see them again,' cried the donkey
staring after the dancing garment. He kicked up his
heels and brayed loudly and then galloped after them
with his teeth bared.

'Hee-haw! Hee-haw! Stop! Stop!' he blared in
his trumpet voice. But he couldn't catch them either,
so he returned to his thistles, hee-hawing at the plight
of poor Sam Pig.

The trousers were now running across a cornfield,
and as they leapt over the stubble Sam was sure there
was somebody inside them. It was an airy fellow,
whose long transparent arms and sea-green fingers
waved and pointed to sky and earth. A laughing mock-
ing face with puffed-out cheeks nodded at Sam, and a
pursed-up mouth whistled shrilly. Wild locks of hair
streamed from the wind's head. The thin eldritch
voice shrieked like pipes playing, wailing and crying,
now high, now low.

'Catch me! Catch me! Get me if you can! I'm the wind, Sam Pig. The wind! I'm the wind from the World's End. From the caves by the mad ocean, from the mountains snow-topped I come. I've flown a thousand leagues to play with you, Sam Pig! Catch me!'

'Wait a minute,' said Sam, rather crossly, and he trundled along on his fat little legs.

The wind turned round and danced about Sam, pulling his tail and blowing in his face so that the little pig had to shut his eyes. Suddenly the wind blew a hurricane. It picked him up and carried him in the air. How frightened was our little Sam Pig when he felt his feet paddling on nothing! His curly tail stuck out straight, his ears were flattened, his body cold as ice. He tried to call for help but no words came. Breathlessly he flew with his legs outstretched, his little feet pad-padding on the soft cushion of air.

Then the wind took pity on him, and dropped him lightly to the ground. He gave a pitiful squeak and lay panting and puffing with fright. He opened his eyes and saw his trousers lying near. He edged towards them and put out a hand, but the trousers stood up, shook themselves full of air, and went dancing off.

Sam Pig arose and followed after. He was a strong-hearted little pig and he was determined not to lose his beloved trousers.

The wind carried them to the farmyard, and sent them fluttering their flapping sides among the hens. The cock crowed, the hens all ran helter-skelter, and the trousers trotted here and there among them, ruffling their feathers, blowing them about like leaves. Sam Pig scrambled over the gate and ran to them, trying to catch the elusive trousers, but getting the cock's tail instead.

'Stop it! Catch it! Catch the wind!' cried Sam.

'Nobody can catch the wind,' crowed the cock. 'Cockadoodle doo! Take shelter, my little red wives!' And the little hens crouched together in a bunch.

'Puff! Puff! Whoo-oo-oo!' screamed the wind, blowing out its cheeks, and prancing in the little check trousers belonging to Sam Pig.

'Quick! Catch it!' called Sam lustily, and he puffed and blew and scampered on aching little legs trying to get the wind, as it whirled round the farm-yard.

The wind blew in a sudden gust and the trousers flew over the gate into the field where the cattle grazed.

'Boo-hoo-oo-oo-oo,' it howled, and it raced round

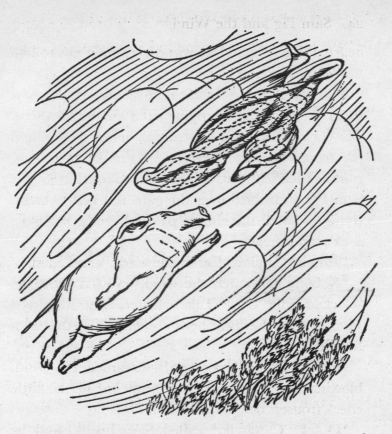

the field blowing the cows so that they fled to the walls and stood within the shelter. But the pair of trousers with the wind inside leapt to the back of a young heifer and sat astride, puffing into her hairy ears, holding her horns with long thin fingers.

She leapt forward in a fright and the wind rode on her backbone, standing on one leg, like a circus rider.

After her went Sam Pig calling, 'Stop! Catch the wind! Give me my trousers!'

'You can't catch the wind, Sam Pig,' mooed the cows from their shelter. 'You can hide till it's past but you can't catch it.'

Down from the cow's back leapt the trousers, and away they jigged and pranced over the grass, twirling at a great pace, with Sam Pig's little legs plodding faithfully after. He was running so fast his legs seemed to twinkle, but the wind went faster, and the trousers now rose in the air like a kite and now paddled over the ground, luring Sam on by pretending to droop and die.

In the next field was Sally the mare. With a whoop and a cry the wind seized her mane and dragged at her long tail. She turned her back and even when the little trousers leapt to her haunches, she took no notice.

'Get on! Gee-up! Whoo-oo-oo to you,' cried the wind, angrily kicking her ribs with invisible toes, and thumping her sides with the empty legs of the check trousers. The mare stood stock still, head bent, eyes closed, refusing to budge an inch. Sam Pig came hurrying up to his old friend.

'Oh Sally! Catch the wind! Keep the wind from taking my trousers away. Hold it, Sally!'

'You can't catch the wind, little Sam. It's free to blow where it likes, and nobody can tame it,' muttered Sally. 'But I won't move for any wind that blows.'

So the wind leapt away and skipped across the fields. The long grasses all turned with it, and tried to follow, but the earth held them back. The trees bent their boughs and the leaves tugged and broke from the twigs and flew after the swift-moving wind.

'There goes the wind,' cried the trees, and they stretched their green fingers in the way the wind had gone.

The wind blew next along a country lane, and the little trousers scampered between the flowery banks with Sam Pig following after. They reached the high road, and Sam hesitated a moment, for he never went alone on the King's Highway. But he was determined to catch his check trousers. Clouds of white dust rose and came after them, pieces of paper were caught and whirled in the air, and a poor butterfly was torn from its flower and swept in the whirlpool of motion after the flying trousers with the wind inside them.

An old woman walked along the road. Her shawl was tightly wrapped around her shoulders, her bonnet fastened with a ribbon, and her black shoes latched on her feet. In her hand she grasped a green umbrella of prodigious size. It was the old witch woman going to the village to do her marketing.

'Drat the wind! It's raising a mighty dust! It will spoil my best bonnet,' she murmured to herself as she saw the cloud of white dust sweeping upon her. She opened the big umbrella and held it over her bonnet. But the wind shot out a long arm and grasped the green umbrella. It snatched it from her hand and bore it away inside out.

She gave a cry of dismay and bent her head to keep her bonnet from being torn from its ribbons. She clutched her shawl and shut her eyes which watered with the dust.

'My poor old umbereller! It's gone! It's seen many a storm of wind and rain, but never a gust as sharp as this!'

The wind passed on, and she ventured to raise her eyes. In the distance she could see the green umbrella flying along, and a pair of trousers running under it, and after them a short fat pig.

'Poor crittur!' she cried. 'A little pig, and it looks like my own friend little Pigwiggin as came to see me once on a time! He's blown away by this terrible varmint of a wind!'

The wind and Sam came to a church with a weathercock on top of the tower. The iron cock looked down in alarm. It spun round on its creaking axis, and crackled its stiff feathers. Backward went the wind, and back went the weathercock, groaning with pain, and back went Sam Pig, and back went the trousers and the umbrella and all. Away they went over the fields, taking the shortest cut, over the brook and up the hill. Sam Pig saw that the wind was heading, or legging, for home. His own little legs were tired and bleeding, his feet were sore, and his eyes red with dust and wind, but he kept on.

There was the little house at the edge of the wood, and there the little stream with Ann filling the kettle, and there the drying-ground with the clothes-line, empty and forlorn between the crab-apple trees.

The wind bustled over the grass and stopped dead. The pair of trousers fell in a heap. The green umbrella lay with its ribs sticking out. Its horn handle and thick cotton cover were unharmed for it had lived a hundred years already and weathered many a gale.

'Give me back my trousers,' said Sam, in a tired little voice.

'Take thy trousers,' answered the wind, and it shook the trousers and dropped them again.

Sam Pig leapt with a last great effort upon his trousers, and held them down. They never offered to move, for the wind had died away, and the air was still.

'Where are you, wind? Where have you gone?' asked Sam when he recovered himself sufficiently to speak. There was silence except for a faint whisper near the ground. Sam put his ear to a hare-bell's lip,

and from it came the clear tiny tinkle of a baby wind which was curled up inside and going to sleep.

'Good-bye, Sam Pig,' said this very small whisper of a voice. 'Good-bye. I gave you a fine run, Sam Pig, and you were a good follower.'

'Good-bye, wind,' murmured Sam, and he sighed and lay down with his head on his trousers. He fell asleep in a twinkling.

There Ann found him when she came to the orchard to collect the clothes-pegs. On the ground lay Sam, with his face coated with dust, but smiling happily. His little feet were stained and cut, his arm outstretched over his torn trousers. By him was a green umbrella, inside out, a gigantic umbrella which would shelter all the family of pigs and badger too, if they sat under it.

Ann carefully turned it the right way. Then she stooped and gave her brother a shake.

'Sam! Sam! Wake up!' she called. 'Sam! Where have you been?'

Sam rubbed his eyes and yawned. Then he sat up.

'Oh Sam! There was such a wind as you never saw! It blew the clothes off the line and I found them lying here, all except your trousers. Oh, poor Sam! I thought it had blown them right away, but here they are, under your head.'

'Yes, Ann,' said Sam, yawning again. 'The wind carried them off. I saw it with my own eyes. It ran a long, long way, but I ran too, and I caught it and got my trousers back again.'

'You caught the wind? You got your trousers back from the raging, roaring wind?' asked Ann in astonishment.

'Yes,' Sam nodded proudly, and he opened his mouth, and shut it again. 'I ran about a hundred miles. I raced the wind, and I wouldn't let it keep my trousers.'

'And what's this?' asked Ann, holding up the green umbrella.

'Oh, that belongs to the nice old witch woman. I passed her on the way, and the wind snatched it from her. I'll take it back some time. I'm so sleepy, Ann. Do leave me alone.'

Sam's head dropped on the trousers, and he fell fast asleep. So Badger carried him in and put him to bed. Ann mended the adventurous trousers which the wind had torn. She turned out the pockets and found a small ancient whistle, which somebody had left there.

'Don't touch it,' warned Badger. 'Don't blow it. It's the wind's own whistle. Don't you know the saying, "Whistle for the wind"? If ever Sam wants the wind to come he has only to blow the whistle. We don't want it now, but if ever we do it will come.'

He put the whistle in a safe place on a top shelf, and there it lay for many a day, forgotten by everybody.

'It's an ill wind that blows nobody good,' observed Bill wisely. 'That long run has made young Sam as slim as a sapling. It is remarkable what a difference the wind makes to a fat little pig's figure.'

'But it was a good run,' said Tom. 'To think that our little Sam caught the wind.'

'Nobody else could do that,' said Ann. They were all very proud of little Sam Pig.

Sam Pig and the Dragon

Of course Sam Pig had always believed that Dragons were extinct, like Unicorns and Ogres. Otherwise he would never have entered Dragon Wood. It was a pretty little wood, filled with primroses and bluebells in the spring, and many birds nested in the trees. Nobody knew why it was called Dragon Wood, and even old Badger laughed at the name. Butterfly Wood, or Dragonfly Wood seemed more suitable for such a charming spot, for many brilliant butterflies flitted among the open spaces, and green dragonflies hovered and darted over the little pond. Sam often went there with his net, but either the meshes were too large or the gossamer threads of the net were too fragile, the little flying creatures always broke away.

One day he went to the wood with a basket for primroses. They grew in clusters under the shade of the rocks, and he soon filled the little rush basket. Then he sat down on a convenient rock. It was rough and black, but ferns grew in the crevices, and lichens patched the surface in orange coloured discs, like coins

spilled over it. The sun had warmed it, and Sam lay back staring at the blue sky, watching the clouds through the young leaves of the overhanging trees. He shut his eyes and let the sun beat down in its spring warmth upon him. He was filled with content, and he was nearly asleep when he was startled by a slight movement under his body. The rock seemed to rise and fall in slow even motion.

He sprang up alarmed, and looked round. There was nothing unusual. The rock lay there, dark and massive, the ferns glowed like transparent green water, the clouds floated in the sky above. Only one thing was different. A little disturbed earth had fallen upon the mossy ground near the rock, and the primroses had spilled from the basket.

Sam Pig rose slowly to his feet. 'I think it was an earthquake,' he said to himself.

He listened, holding his breath, and there came a deep sigh. Perhaps it was a sigh, perhaps it was the wind moaning. Then he thought he saw an eye flash at him. Perhaps it was an eye, perhaps it was the sun in the glittering rain pool. Sam didn't wait any longer. He picked up the basket, stuffed the primroses in it, and went home. He turned his head now and then, and saw nothing alarming, but he couldn't help wondering.

'I've been to Dragon Wood,' he announced when he entered the house. 'And I heard – and I felt – and I saw '

'Well?' cried Tom impatiently. 'What did you hear and feel and see? A dragonfly?'

'Nothing,' said Sam, hesitating. Then he added, 'But it was like something. A nothing that was like something.'

He didn't go near Dragon Wood again for months. He stayed away till the flowers had gone and the trees were beginning to change the colour of their leaves.

'I want some blackberries for jam,' said Ann one autumn day. 'Go to Dragon Wood and pick some, Sam. There's plenty on those bushes, and nobody ever goes there.'

'Dragon Wood,' said Sam slowly. 'Dragon Wood. Well –. Yes, I'll go, Ann. I'll take my fiddle for company. I feel a bit queersome in Dragon Wood when I'm all alone.'

'All right. Take your fiddle, Sam. Maybe you will wheedle the blackberries off the bushes by playing to them, and I'm sure the rabbits will enjoy your music,' laughed Ann.

So away went Sam. There were the finest black-berries on a bank where the trees were scarce, and the rocks broke through the earth. He picked the juicy fruit and filled the little basket, and ate a good few himself. Then he put the basket under a tree and wandered on with his fiddle under his chin, playing a tune as he walked. The wood seemed to listen, the birds cocked their heads and sang in reply, the trees waved their branches in slow lazy rhythm, and Sam Pig felt happy and carefree. He saw the rock which had once moved and there it was, solid as the earth, weather worn and black with rain. Yet when he stared at it he thought it was somehow different. He could trace a kind of shape about it, a bulging forehead, heavy brows, and even eyelids, long slits cut deep in the rock, half covered with bright moss. He didn't feel inclined to sit upon it, but he went on playing, to make himself brave.

Now whether it was the sweetness of Sam's music, or the warmth of the autumn sun, I do not know, but the bracken began to wave, the earth quivered and shook, and the rock was slowly uplifted. It was a scaly dark head, very large and long, with half-shut eyes concealing a glimmer of light like stars in a cloud. Ferns and lichens rolled away, the little silver birch trees toppled over, and a large oak-tree crashed to the ground as the huge beast stretched itself. Then it opened its mouth and yawned, and it was as if a pit had opened in the wood. Sam gave a shrill cry and backed away. The Dragon blinked its liquid eyes and looked at Sam. The glance was kindly, and Sam stopped.

'Hallo,' said the Dragon, in a voice which seemed to come from under the earth, so deep and rumbling it was. 'Hallo, I've been asleep I think! What time is it?'

'About twelve o'clock,' said Sam in a shaking voice, and he glanced up at the sun. 'Yes. About twelve.'

'What day?' asked the Dragon, after a long pause.

'It's Saturday,' faltered Sam.

'I mean, what year,' said the Dragon, very, very slowly. 'It's always Saturday. What year is it?'

'Oh, it's – er – nineteen hundred and something,' stammered Sam. 'I can't remember what.'

'Too soon,' growled the Dragon, like low thunder. 'Too soon. I've waked too early. I had to sleep till twenty hundred.'

'When did you go to bed?' asked Sam, forgetting his fright in his curiosity.

'Oh, in the year a hundred or thereabouts. The Romans made it so uncomfortable for me, marching about with their legions and tidying everywhere, I went to sleep and covered myself up. But I've waked too soon. My sleeping time is two thousand years. Have they gone yet?'

'Who?' asked Sam.

'The Romans,' said the Dragon.

'I'm not sure,' said Sam. 'But there's only me and Badger and my brothers and sister Ann living near. Not any Romans.'

The Dragon seemed to ponder this, and there was a long silence.

'Hadn't you better go back to bed again?' asked Sam, staring uneasily at the great head. 'I'll cover you up.'

'Now I'm awake I'll just look about me,' said the Dragon. 'I like your music, young fellow. Play to me again.'

The Dragon yawned once more and showed its long white teeth and its curving scarlet tongue. A faint blue smoke came from its nostrils, and it blinked and snorted.

'I can't breathe properly,' it grumbled. 'Play to me. My throat's sore. I must have got a chill in the damp ground. I expect it's been raining and snowing a bit while I've been sleeping there. I hope I shan't get rheumatics.'

Sam played his fiddle and the Dragon waved its head in slow awkward jerks, up and down, stretching its scaly folds, loosening the thick stony skin.

'That's better,' said the Dragon. 'You've done me good. I am not so stiff now, and my throat's more comfortable.'

Sam thought it was time he went home, but the Dragon had taken a liking to him. So when he started off, the Dragon followed after. Sam quite forgot his blackberries, and he walked quickly, not caring to run from the great beast. The Dragon scarcely seemed to move, but it arrived as soon as Sam.

'You'd best wait outside,' said Sam. 'They'll be a bit surprised when they see you. I'd better warn them. You see, you are too big to come into our house. We're not used to Dragons, but I'm sure everybody will be pleased to see you.'

The Dragon agreed, and it lay down in the field.

'I am much obliged to you,' it murmured in its deep rumble. 'I can breathe easily now. The change of position has done me good, and the ancient warmth inside me has wakened.'

Indeed it had! From its nostrils came a cloud of smoke and from its mouth spurted little flickering flames of fire.

'You're burning,' cried Sam. 'Shall I fetch some water from the spring?'

The Dragon shook its great head, knocking over the palings and the clothes-props in the crab-apple orchard. 'I never drink water. It puts me out. It's my nature to smoke. You'll get used to it.'

So Sam ran up the garden path and flung open the door. He was breathless with excitement. 'Ann! Tom! Bill!' he shouted. 'There's a Dragon outside.'

'Dragon!' scoffed Bill. 'Where are the black-

berries? We've been waiting to make the jam. Why
have you been so long?'

'There's a Dragon outside,' repeated Sam. 'I forgot the blackberries because I found a Dragon. I've
brought it home with me. At least,' he corrected himself, not wishing to appear boastful, 'at least, it
followed me. It's waiting outside.'

They stared in amazement at their young brother,
and then they ran to the door. They could see the
monster lying outside the garden gate, with its
head in the lane and its tail in the paddock. Little
spirals of smoke came from the Dragon's nostrils,
and its green eyes stared unblinkingly from the rocky
head.

'Now, Sam,' said Ann, crossly, 'whatever did you
bring a Dragon home for? You went for blackberries,
not Dragons. What shall we do with it? We haven't a
stable for it, and we can't have it in the house.'

'Stable! House!' scoffed Tom. 'If it whisks its
long tail our house will be knocked clean over, and if
it moves its head the orchard will be destroyed. It is
singeing the crab-apples already.'

'It may ripen the crabs,' said Sam eagerly. 'It's
very warm.'

'If it breathes hard we shall be roasted into roast
pork,' said Bill, mournfully.

'But it's a nice gentle Dragon,' interrupted Sam, 'and I found it. I think it is lonely.'

'Well, go and speak to it,' said Tom, shrugging his shoulders.

Sam went down the garden to talk to the Dragon. It lay very still, breathing quietly, staring at the blue sky.

'You had best stay outside,' said Sam, 'and please behave yourself, for Sister Ann is rather worried about you.'

The Dragon nodded so hard that Sam was blown backward by the force of the wind. It promised to behave if only Sam Pig would let it stay. It curled itself round the house and garden, and shut its eyes.

Then the rest of the Pig family went closer to look at it. Its head was near the garden gate, but not near enough to scorch it. Its tail swept under the wall, and away into the orchard. There was just room to walk past without getting harmed by the Dragon's breath. They agreed it was quite a nice beast, and very unusual.

Badger was much surprised when he came home that evening. He hummed and hawed as Sam told the exciting story. The Dragon was dozing, and Badger watched it.

'It belongs to an ancient family,' said Brock. 'It is

probably the last one left in the land. It will be lonely without companions. It's a pity you waked it, Sam. It may cause us a deal of trouble. I'm not used to Dragons.'

'I am,' said Sam. 'It likes my music, and it's quite tame. Let us keep it, Badger. I will be its companion.'

The little Pig looked imploringly at Brock, and Brock hummed a little tune and gazed at the Dragon. It was rather awkward having that great hot beast so near to one's garden gate. Nobody would come to visit them, but of course it was as good as having a watchdog. In any case Brock didn't know how to get rid of the Dragon. There it was and there it would stay.

They soon got used to having a Dragon round the house. It was very tame and gentle, and no trouble at all. The little animals of the woodland played on its scaly back, rabbits leapt upon it, and robins perched on its eyelids. The Dragon lay very still, just breathing, opening an eye now and then when Sam played to it, smiling at the little pig.

Ann Pig stretched a clothes-line over its head, from the lilac tree in the garden to the wild sloe in the orchard. Then she hung out the washing to dry in the fire of the Dragon's breath. The clothes dried even in wet weather, which was a great saving of time and

trouble. The crab-apples ripened, the flowers sprang
up anew in the hothouse of the Dragon's presence.
When the days were short and winter came, the
Dragon kept the house as warm as toast. The snow
fell and the frosts made the earth like iron, but the
Dragon lay there, a warm comforting beast. They sat
on its back in the coldest weather, and picnicked on

the moss-covered scaly tail. The Dragon told them stories of long ago, tales of the days when wolves and wild boars and shaggy bears lived in the country. It told them of its brother Dragons, and its ancient mother, famous throughout the world for her strength. Then a tear of loneliness would trickle down its face, a tear so hot that steam rose from it. Sam rose to fetch his fiddle to cheer the sad beast, and the Dragon sighed and winked away the tears, and forgot its ancient greatness.

Brock brought his friends to see the wonderful visitor and everyone said the pigs were honoured by this King of Reptiles who was so considerate and kind.

Spring came, and Sam sat on the garden gate with his fiddle. The cuckoo called and the nightingale sang. The Dragon moved its head in its sleepy bliss, and puffed the white smoke from its nostrils, and the yellow flames from its mouth. It was always content, never asking for anything, neither eating nor drinking, – a perfect guest.

Then one fine day a cow disappeared. Sam Pig had seen it coming up the lane, and he ran indoors to fetch his milking-pail and the three-legged stool. When he came out the cow wasn't there, so the pigs had no milk for their tea. It was very strange, and

Sam hunted in the fields for the lost cow. She had completely vanished.

A few days later another cow went. She had been feeding in the meadow, near the Dragon's tail. The farmer's dog came to look for her, and he eyed the Dragon suspiciously. The Dragon's eyes were shut, and the great beast lay with a look of happiness on its stony face.

The sheep-dog spoke to the pig family. 'It's my opinion,' said he, sternly, 'it's my good opinion that that there Dragon knows something about our Nancy. Aye, and about our Primrose too, as went the other day. She was a good milker was Nancy. Well, you can't have it both ways. You can't keep a Dragon, and have your gallon of milk regular.'

'It can't be the Dragon,' protested Sam. 'Why, there's a blackbird's nest on its back, and there's a brood of young rabbits living beneath it. Everybody knows our Dragon, and it's as gentle as a dove.'

'That's as may be,' returned the dog. 'I'm only telling you. I've my suspicions. Cows can't fade away like snow in summer.'

The pigs talked it over and Sam decided to sit on the Dragon's back and keep watch. The Dragon never noticed who was on its back, it was too thick-skinned to feel any difference. Sam had once seen the roadman empty a cartload of stone upon it when he was mending the lane, but the Dragon never flinched. Only the carthorse shied, and was restive till he was led away.

So Sam sat light as a feather on the Dragon's back, and kept guard. He felt he was acting the traitor's part to his friend, and he carried his fiddle ready to play a tune to soothe the Dragon's feelings if he had misjudged it.

Up the road came a cow, going to the milking. It loitered here and there, picking up a blade of grass, snuffling at the herbage. When it got to the Dragon it put out its red tongue and licked the salty scales of the beast. Sam waited breathlessly. The Dragon snapped open its mouth, and in a twinkling the cow had gone. Like a flash it shot down the flaming red lane of the Dragon's throat.

'That settles it,' said Sam quietly, and he slid to the ground, and went round to face the Dragon.

'You'd best be going back to bed, Dragon,' said he in a determined way, but the Dragon opened its sleepy eyes and gazed lovingly at Sam.

'Not yet, Sam dear,' said the Dragon. 'Not yet. I'm so happy where I am, dear Sam Pig.'

Sam was not to be cajoled. He took his fiddle and played a marching song.

'Follow me,' he commanded the Dragon. 'Fall in and follow me. Quick march! One! Two! One! Two!'

The Dragon stirred its great length, heaved its heavy body from the orchard and meadow grass, and shuffled after Sam.

Back to Dragon Wood Sam led the Dragon. He took it right to the place where he had found it. There was the hollow, where its head had lain, and the wide ditch where its body had rested.

'Now go to sleep,' said Sam. 'I'll play a lullaby, and you must shut your eyes and go fast asleep.'

Sam played a gentle rocking tune and the Dragon gazed at Sam. A great warm tear rolled down the Dragon's cheek, and then another tear fell with a splash on the ground. The Dragon shut its eyes obediently and settled itself in the moist earth. Soon there was no movement in the vast body. The Dragon was asleep.

Sam covered it up with leaves and grasses and planted ferns and spring flowers upon its back. Then he turned and looked at it. Only a great black rock stuck out from the earth, with little silver birch-trees waving their branches near. There was no trace of a Dragon in the wood.

Sam stroked the rugged surface of the rock, and

then he went sadly home. Many a time he returned to Dragon Wood, and climbed on the dark rock, to visit his ancient friend. He played and sang and talked to the Dragon, but there was never a movement. Not till the year two thousand or thereabouts would the Dragon waken again.

Sam Pig and the Cuckoo Clock

On the mantelpiece in the house of the four pigs stood a clock. It was an ordinary kind of a clock, with a white face covered with a glass window, a brass pendulum and a hole for winding up the works. It was Badger's duty as head of the household to wind it, and nobody else ever dared to touch it. There it stood between Badger's herb-baccy box and the money-box with the slit for pence. Every night Badger lifted it down and opened the glass window. He took the key from its hook and then wound up the clock with a whirring clicking noise which always pleased little Sam Pig.

'Can I have a go, Brock? Can I wind up the clock? Can I look inside at the works?' he implored, but Brock shook his head.

'Nobody must wind it but me, for clocks are ticklish creatures, and they don't like clumsy paws meddling with their innards.'

The clock ticked with a cheerful sound, and the four pigs loved to listen to the familiar voice, saying

'Tick tock,' night and day, and to watch the little brass pendulum which they could see through the glass window. It seemed to talk to them, to say, 'Now it's time to put the potatoes in the hot ashes to cook for dinner,' or 'Now it's time to fill the kettle for tea.' They ran to obey.

When Badger went away for his winter's sleep the clock stopped, just as if it were lonely without him. The little pigs looked up at the white face, and listened for the tick, but the hands said 'A quarter to five', and they never moved day or night. Two friends were gone, Brock and the clock, and they missed them. When Badger returned, the first thing he did was to wind up the clock and start the little wagging pendulum. Then the clock called, 'Here I am! Here I am!' and the four pigs rejoiced.

Of course there were plenty of ways of telling the time besides the clock, but they were quiet ways. There was the sun moving majestically across the sky from East to West, sending shadows which got shorter and shorter till midday when they were the shortest. Then they began to lengthen till the sun went down. Badger put a stick in the garden and showed the family how to tell the time by it. He pointed to the stick's black shadow, which stretched across the grass early in the day. At twelve o'clock it became only a very tiny fellow. 'The sun is the best clock of all,' said Brock. But sometimes the sun didn't shine and then there were no shadows.

Ann Pig said a good way to know the time was to pick a dandelion clock and blow the little white seedlings. 'One, two, three, four,' she puffed, and away flew the parasols to make new dandelions in the garden ready for salad.

Sam Pig liked a ticking clock, one that struck the hours and told everybody the time. He liked the brassy voice, and the loud call. So when the clock stopped and nobody was allowed to wind it up, Sam was very sad.

One day he climbed on a chair and reached for the clock. He fitted the key in the hole and turned it with a grinding noise. Clicketty Click went the clock, and Sam pressed it to his chest and dragged the key round and round with all his strength. He went on turning for a long time, and the clock didn't like the pain in its stomach. When Sam put the clock down there was a whirring buzz, and it began to strike. One, two, three, four, five, it went on striking all the hours and many more. It went into tomorrow and the next day. The hands whirled round and the clock ticked so madly that nobody knew what it said.

Ann was in a terrible fright when she heard it

chattering like a cageful of magpies. Bill said the clock was saying, 'You shouldn't have done it. You shouldn't have done it. You shouldn't have done it.' Tom said that Badger would rage when he came home.

All the pigs ran about very fast, trying to go to bed, to get up, to eat and cook and do the work, but they couldn't keep up with the hastening clock. Ann was breathless, and Sam didn't know where he was. Tom burnt the dinner and let the kettle boil dry. The fire flared up in a fury, and the sticks crackled and spat. Everyone was in such a hurry and such a confusion that they fell on top of each other.

Only Bill sat in a corner watching the whirling fingers of the clock.

'It can't go on for ever like this,' he told them calmly, when Ann cried to him to hurry for it was tomorrow fortnight. 'It will be the end of the world soon, so we may as well take it easy while we can.'

'The end of the world?' Ann burst into tears. 'I won't have my end of the world without Brock,' she sobbed.

Then Sam went into the garden, scampering out and scampering in at double speed.

'The shadow-stick is moving quite slowly,' said he. 'The sun isn't running across the sky. It's the same as usual. It's only today. I think something's going to happen to this clock.'

Sure enough, the clock struck one thousand, one hundred and one. It whirred and buzzed and chuffed. Then it was silent. Never was there such a silence. The four pigs stood staring, motionless. The birds in the garden stopped singing, and even the wind was quiet as if it couldn't understand what had happened in the house of the four pigs.

Then everyone began to talk. The birds sang, the wind whistled and all the pigs shouted, 'It's broken. Time has stopped.' They asked each other what Badger would say! They were very much upset! They looked inside the clock and touched its snapped springs, and its toothed wheels and its slim fingers.

'We had best get another clock before Brock comes home,' said Bill.

'But where shall we find one?' asked Tom.

'We are the only family that has a clock,' said Ann.

'And there may not be another in all the world,' said Bill.

'Oh, yes! I've seen clocks on church towers,' interrupted Sam eagerly. 'When I was with Man we used to look up at the church towers. We listened to their striking bells and we could see their long fingers jerk along.'

'All right, Sam. You'd best get a clock from a church tower,' said Tom, coldly. 'You broke our clock, and you seem to know all about them. You go and get one.'

Sam's face fell. 'I can't climb a church tower,' he explained. 'It's miles and miles high, and when you get to the top the church clock is as big as a house.

We could all live inside a clock like that, but we should be deafened by the striking.'

'That's your affair,' said Bill crossly. 'You broke the clock and you must get another from somewhere.'

'Yes. That's fair enough,' said Tom. Only Ann was sorry for the little pig who stood looking so disconsolate.

'Never mind, Sam,' she whispered. 'I'll say a word to Brock and he will forgive you.'

'Forgiving won't give us back our clock,' said Bill, who overheard. 'Now, Ann, leave him alone. He must go off and find a clock.'

'And he mustn't come back with a dandelion clock either,' added Tom, sternly.

So Sam packed his pyjamas in his knapsack, and a piece of soap and a toothbrush with them. Ann gave him a rock bun and a clean handkerchief, and away he went clock-hunting.

But clocks don't grow on oak-trees, and although Sam searched high and low in the woods he couldn't find anything like a clock. The Jay watched him and hopped from bough to bough of the trees to try to find what Sam Pig was looking for. The wood pigeons called, 'Tak two coos, Sam. Tak two coos,' but that didn't help. The cuckoo called, 'Cuckoo. Cuckoo,' and flew over Sam's head.

'Has anybody seen a clock?' called Sam Pig, but the birds only whistled and sang with joy because Spring had come with the cuckoo.

So Sam Pig sat down and ate his cake and thought it over. He couldn't go back without a clock, so he decided to go to an old friend for advice. He decided to visit the old witch, who, you may remember, wasn't a witch at all, but an old woman who lived alone in the wood.

That was a good plan, he was sure, and he sprang to his feet and started off through the long deep woods towards the little cottage. It was late at night when he arrived, but the old woman had a candle burning in her window and a bright fire blazing on her hearth. The light of it flickered down the wood among the trees, and Sam hastened to the garden and up to the door. He tapped and waited.

'Come in. Come in, whoever you may be,' said the witch.

'Why, it's my little Pigwiggin come to see me again,' she cried when Sam pushed open the door and stepped into the room, blinking at the light.

She threw her arms round Sam Pig and kissed him on the nose. That was the second kiss Sam had had in his life.

'How are you, little Pigwiggin?' she cried.

Sam said he was very well, only tired and hungry. So she gave him supper and aired his pyjamas, and all the time she talked to him about her Owlet and her cat. The Owlet was now full grown, she told Sam, and he no longer rode on her shoulder, he was too heavy. He sat on a chair and stared with round eyes at Sam Pig. As for the cat she turned her back and took no notice whatever.

'And what brings you here?' asked the old woman at last when Sam had said nothing. 'I hope you haven't run away from home.'

'No, although I sometimes want to when Bill and Tom are angry with me,' said Sam fiercely. 'No. They turned me out.'

'What? Packed you off into the wide world?'

'Yes. They sent me away,' said Sam.

'But why? What have you done?' asked the witch, sorrowfully.

'I broke our clock,' said Sam, 'and they sent me out to find another.'

Then he told how he had wound up Badger's clock, which went buzzing along till it broke.

'Do you know where I can find a clock?' asked Sam. 'I came to ask you, because you are the wisest person I know, except Brock.'

He looked anxiously at the witch over the edge of

his bowl of milk. There was a comforting ticking sound in the room, and he knew the witch had a clock for he had seen it on his first visit.

'You've come to the right place, Pigwiggin,' said the witch. 'I've got a clock I never use, for it makes such a to-do, such a chatter, I get weary of it. I want to be quiet in my old age. You shall have it with pleasure, for there is the old grandfather clock in the corner, and he keeps me company. I don't want my little noisy clock.'

Sam thanked her over and over again, but she stopped him.

'That's enough, Sam. You've said "Thank you" as often as a striking clock. Say no more but go off to sleep. Tomorrow I will get the clock down from the attic. It's a queer one but it keeps good time, and you can wind it yourself.'

So she made up the bed on the hearthrug, and Sam lay down in his warm pyjamas. Just before he fell asleep he heard the old woman call 'Tirra-lirra', and a mouse ran out of a hole to be fed. Sam smiled sleepily at the Owl and nodded at the sulky cat. Then he shut his eyes and knew no more till morning.

The next day they all had breakfast together of porridge and cream. The porridge had curls of treacle on the top.

'What's this?' asked Sam. 'What is this sweetness that isn't honey?' He had never seen treacle before, of course, for it comes from the sugar-cane, and not from the honeycomb.

'It's treacle, my Pigwiggin,' said the old woman. 'Have you never tasted it before? You shall have a tin to take home with you.'

'It's delicious,' said Sam. 'Even the bees would desert their honey-tree for this tin, I think, and the Fox would run a mile for a taste.'

The old woman nodded and smiled and gave him more till his buttons were nearly bursting off. Then she took him to the garden to see her daffodils and pinks. It was such a warm sunny corner of the forest the flowers all bloomed at once and they kept in blossom till the snows came.

Overhead flew the Jay. 'Witch! Witch!' he shrieked and he swooped down to snatch a crust from the bird-table which the old woman had set for him and his friends.

'Pretty Jay,' she said. 'He comes here every day to see me, and he always speaks so kindly to me.'

Sam Pig frowned at the Jay, and the Jay mocked and jeered at Sam Pig.

But the old woman went back to the house and brought out the clock. It was a most beautiful clock in the shape of a little house, with a window just under the thatched roof, and the clock face over the front door. Two fir cones dangled from beneath it and the old woman showed Sam how to wind it up. She pulled down one fir cone, and the other moved into the house. It was quite easy, and the clock at once began to tick in a loud and cheerful manner.

'Put it under your arm,' said the witch. 'Don't jerk it, but carry it carefully, and when you get home ask your brother to hang it on the wall. It is going now and will tell you the time all the way home.'

Sam thanked her again and away he went, with the clock under one arm and the tin of treacle under the other.

The old woman stood at her gate waving to him till he got out of sight.

'The good little Pigwiggin,' said she to herself.

Sam trotted along towards home, and he hummed a song of happiness because he was carrying a clock for Brock the Badger. The clock ticked loudly against his heart, and the treacle tin sent out a good sweet smell.

'It's a very pretty clock,' said Sam, taking a peep at it. 'They will be surprised when they see it. A house with two fir cones!'

There was a sudden whir and the little window

flew open. Out flew a tiny cuckoo and shouted
'Cuckoo. Cuckoo. Cuckoo,' nine times. Then back it
flew and the window shut and the clock went on
ticking as if nothing had happened.

'Goodness me!' cried Sam, holding the clock at
arm's length. 'There's a cuckoo inside it! And it
knows the time, for it *is* nine o'clock!'

He hurried along the woods, but every hour the
cuckoo came out and sang its merry song and
fluttered its little feathers. Sam tried to catch it, to
make it speak of other things, but the cuckoo flew
back to the dark interior of the clock and shut the
window fast.

'Ho, cuckoo! Stop a minute!' called Sam. 'Let me
in! Open your window! I want to look inside your
house.' He rapped at the door and tapped at the
window, and peered down the chimney, but he could
see nothing.

'Tick tock! Tick tock!' went the clock, and the
house door remained firmly closed.

'Why are you hurrying so fast, Sam Pig?' asked
the Fox, stepping out of the bushes. 'What have you
got there?'

'Nothing for you,' said Sam quickly, and he tried
to push past, but the Fox snatched the clock from
him.

'A house,' said the Fox. 'And who lives in it, Sam? Some honey-bees perhaps. There is a sweet smell about you, Sam Pig.' Sam Pig had pushed the tin of treacle in his pocket, and now he stood waiting.

'Tick tock!' went the clock, very loudly, and then it made a little buzzing noise.

'I think it is going to explode,' said the Fox, holding it at arm's length. 'I think this house is a queer one.'

Out flew the cuckoo, and shouted 'Cuckoo. Cuckoo,' in the Fox's face, and flapped its little wings against his nose.

'The bold bird! Take it back! I don't want such a magical thing. It's a trap or something. You take care, Sam Pig, or that bird will peck your eyes out. It nearly got mine.'

So Sam Pig went home with the cuckoo clock safe and sound, and the Fox ran through the woods to tell his family that Sam Pig had a magical bird in a little magical house, and it would peck your eyes out as soon as winking.

The pigs were delighted when Sam showed them the new clock, and they hung it up on a nail in the kitchen. They all stood listening to the noisy tick tock, and gazing at the little house. The roof was thatched with green reeds, and the little door had a brass knocker. Sam explained that he had knocked and banged at the door and tapped on the window but nobody came out till it was the hour for striking.

'It's four o'clock,' said he. 'Now you shall see for yourselves.'

The window sprang open and out flew the little cuckoo, and called the hour.

It flew round the room, calling 'Cuckoo. Cuckoo!' It blinked its eyes and shook its feathers, and tossed its head and then it returned to the little house.

The pigs could talk of nothing else all evening, and as each hour approached they waited for the bird to come out and sing to them. It was striking eight when Badger entered the room.

'Hallo,' he cried. 'What's this? A little cuckoo flying round? Where has it come from? It's the smallest bird I ever saw in all my life.'

But the bird flicked its tail, called eight times and flew back through its window.

'It's a clock,' said Sam. 'I broke your clock, Brock. This is a new one, from the witch's house. It's a cuckoo clock.'

Brock stood looking at the little house, admiring the neat thatching of the roof, and the overlapping wooden shingles, and the sweet-scented fir cones

which hung from their chains. Then he lifted the
brass knocker and tapped at the tiny door.

'It's no good knocking there,' said Sam. 'It's not a
real door. Nothing happens.'

But even as he spoke the door swung slowly open
and they could all see inside the little house. There
was the cuckoo, sitting in a bare little room, with its

feathers drooping and its shoulders hunched. It glanced at them, and then turned its head away.

'Hush,' said Sam Pig. 'It's going to sleep,' and they closed the door.

But early the next morning Sam Pig slipped down to the kitchen, and waited to see the cuckoo come out. It darted from its window and flew cuckooing out of the door, and into the woods. Away it flew, and it didn't come back for an hour. With it came another cuckoo, small and stiff like itself, with quick bright eyes and grey-barred breast. They both flew in at the little window of the cuckoo clock, and the shutter closed after them.

'There's another cuckoo come to the clock,' said Sam, when Brock came down to breakfast. 'I expect our cuckoo was lonely.'

Brock tapped at the door and pushed it open a crack. There were primroses on the table, and on the hearth a little fire gleamed. Two cuckoos sat talking by the fireside, speaking in low whispering voices.

Brock closed the door silently and nodded to Sam.

'Did you see the little fire burning and the candlestick on the mantelpiece and the primroses?' asked Sam.

'Yes. Look at the smoke coming out of the chimney. The cuckoo is making himself at home.'

Indeed it was so, for a tiny column of blue smoke came curling from the chimney of the wooden house. Every hour the cuckoo came out to call the time, and with him came his wife, two birds which flew round the room and then disappeared into their own little dwelling.

Sam Pig and the Irishmen

The four pigs were awakened by the sound of a mowing-machine in the field across the woods. At breakfast they talked about it.

'Did you hear the mowers at five o'clock this morning?' asked Sam. He helped himself to the cream and
looked round the table at his brothers and sister Ann
and old Brock.

'I should think I did,' said Tom. 'They must be in
Greeny pasture, for that is the nearest mowing field
to us. It sounded quite loud.'

'That's because the air is so still,' said Badger.
'You can hear the whir of a mowing-machine a long
way in the early day, but when Sam gets up you can't
hear anything.'

'Oh, I say, Brock,' cried Sam Pig. 'I don't make a
noise. I'm quiet as a shadow. In fact this morning I
counted five cuckoos and a woodpecker and a corn-
crake as well as the mowing-machine, all rattling and
calling.'

'I expect the Irishmen have come to the farm,'

said Ann, changing the conversation, for Sam looked annoyed with Brock. 'They come every year like the cuckoo, and then the haymaking starts.'

'I like Irishmen,' said Sam. 'I like Irishmen better nor pigs, and better nor a badger.' He spoke defiantly and they all laughed at his frowning face.

'You'd better go and live with them, Sam,' scoffed Bill. 'See if they will have you.'

'Ask them to take you on as a haymaker,' said Brock.

'I'll go,' said Sam. 'Yes. I've always wanted to help with haymaking, and I like Irishmen better nor my brothers.'

'You won't be able to stop in bed, and be lazy if you join them,' said Bill.

'Well, Sam, Irishmen are kind to pigs,' said Brock. 'They are the only people in the world who have sense and know the dignity and the value of a well-bred pig. I expect they will welcome you.'

He spoke soothingly, and Sam was sorry he had been angry with his guardian and friend, old Brock. But he stuck to his word. 'I'll go and see if they will have me. I really do love Irishmen, although I've never known any. I love them next to you, Brock, and better nor Bill and Tom.'

'I'll lend you my old straw hat,' said Ann. 'Hay-

making is hot work and you might get the sunstroke.
Besides your ears will not be so obvious. They are
rather large, Sam.'

Ann fetched her wide straw hat and Sam put it on
his head and tilted it sideways.

'There! What am I like?' he asked.

'A haymaker,' they all replied.

'Take a little present with you,' said Tom. 'I've some nice potatoes, and they'll be welcome among the Irish.'

'And I'll pack a few pasties,' added Ann.

'Mind and behave yourself,' said Bill. 'Irishmen are all gentlemen and they won't let you stay if you are greedy.'

So Sam set off, with his fiddle under his arm, and the bag of potatoes, and pasties and a bottle of herb beer. He carried, too, a little wooden rake which Badger made for him, ready for work. On the way through the woods he met the Fox, who was hanging about looking for anything he could find.

'Hallo, Sam Pig! Where are you off to, with a rake and a fiddle and a bag of something on your back?' said the Fox.

'I'm going haymaking,' said Sam. 'Would you like to come with me?'

'Yes. I love haymaking,' said the Fox. 'When they cut the grass many a family of rabbits comes out, and I love the little dears.'

So Sam and the Fox went along together. The Fox took long strides and Sam padded as fast as he could. His legs got tired trying to keep up with the Fox. So the Fox suggested a rest.

'What's in your bag, Sam?' he asked.

Sam opened it and the Fox helped himself to the pasties and herb beer.

'Surely you were not going to eat all this?' he asked.

'No,' said Sam. 'I was taking it to the Irishmen. I'm going to join them and stay with them. I'm not going home tonight. Oh, no! I'm going to be an Irishman.'

Sam spoke proudly, but the Fox gave a start.

'The Irishmen?' he cried. 'Have they come? Then I don't think I will go with you, Sam Pig.'

'Why not?' asked Sam.

'They don't like me. They call me the little red gentleman, but they won't welcome me. Now you are a favourite of theirs. They will take you to their hearts. I won't come any further.'

So after finishing off Sam's provisions, the Fox went back to the woods and Sam went on alone. At last he came to the field where the mowing-machine was cutting the grass and the haymakers were tedding. Sam climbed the gate and went into the field. He didn't speak, but he quickly put his bag of potatoes under the hedge and he cut himself a forked branch to toss the grass. Then he began to work, with one eye on the three Irishmen in the distance. Their trousers were tied round the legs with wisps of grass, and Sam tied his little check trousers too. Their striped shirts were open at the neck. They wore big hats like Sam's.

'There's a little fellow come to help us,' said one. 'Glory be, but he's the smallest little chap I've seed outside a show.'

'He's got a nose on him, and a pair of ears like our pig in the cabin in Galway,' said another.

'Hi there!' hailed the third. 'Come here, little fellow, and let us take a look at you. What's your name?'

'Sam Pig,' replied Sam, going up to them. 'And I've brought you a bag of taters, and if you'll let me help you, I'll do my best.'

'Begorra! It *is* a pig! Well, and isn't this homely? We've not seen such a fat little gossoon since we left old Ireland's shores. Come along and help us, Sam.'

They slapped Sam's back and laughed among themselves at the little pig, and put him to ted the grass. So Sam followed them up and down the great field, and talked to them as they worked.

They told him their names were Malachi, and Pat, and Jimmy, and each of them had a nice little pig at home, just the size of Sam.

It was very nice to talk to them, and to hear their grand Irish voices, and to sniff their baccy and their good Irish smell of peat and other odorous things.

Sam thought Brock would enjoy being with them, but when he mentioned his friend they shook their heads. Nay, they didn't want no Badgers. Pigs were friendly and good to have in a cabin, but not Badgers.

'My Brock is different,' said Sam, staunchly. But they all laughed at him in a joyful way, and took off his straw hat and put it back to front, and gave him a scrap of twist to chew and a sup of beer to drink. Sam felt rather dizzy, but he was determined to do whatever his new friends said was right.

At dinner time he followed them to the farm shed, where they had their dwelling. There were sacks of straw for them to sleep upon, and a long table where they sat for their meals. It was all very comfortable and homely for little Sam.

A farm man came in to talk to the Irishmen, and Sam kept to the shadows.

'I see you've got a helper,' said the man, staring curiously at Sam. 'Friend of yours?'

'Yes. He's a small bit of an Irishman, and he doesn't want any wages. He's working for love of us. If you just bring a bite and sup for him that is all he wants,' said Malachi.

So a bite and sup were brought for Sam Pig, and he ate in his corner, and listened to the brave talk.

In the afternoon Jimmy told him to rest in the hay,

but Sam refused. He had come to work in the hayfield, and he would stick it. Sally the mare was grazing in the next field, which was pasture land, and she put her head over the hedge to have a word with Sam Pig.

'You're a bold fellow, Sam,' she remarked. 'It's a caution you are, coming to the haunts of men, and waving your hayfork and drinking your tot of beer like the haymakers. Aren't you afeard?'

'No,' whispered Sam. 'They are Irishmen, and they are friends. They would never betray me. Not like that Man who carried me off! Why, Malachi and Jimmy and Pat call me Pigwiggin, they do, and they treat me like their own brother.'

'Well, Sam. Are you getting tired?' asked Jimmy, who was working near. 'There's a drop of tea coming, and it will put new life in you. Let's sit under this oak-tree and rest a bit.'

The others came up and the men drank their tea and took a bite of barm cake and Sam had his share. Then he showed them his fiddle, and he tuned up and played a lively air.

Jimmy whistled an Irish jig and Sam played the tune. They were delighted with little Sam, and they gave him high praise. But work had to go on, till the stars came out. Sam squatted on a haycock and watched the lively scenes around him. Over the road was the farmhouse, with people coming and going, men leading horses to water, cows to the milking. The pigs were squealing in the sty, and the hens came clucking to the field to have a chat with Sam. Ducks waddled across the corner from the pond, and a great turkey gobbled and strutted. Sam Pig sat on his mound of hay, a king among them all.

'What a tale to tell Brock!' he said to himself. 'What a lot of adventures I have had! And the folk I have met, and the farm food I have eaten, and the great fine company of the Irishmen! Never have I had such a day!'

But he yawned sleepily, and would have gone fast asleep if the Irishmen had not called to him to get ready. The hens were running back for their supper of corn, and the turkey was strolling to the barn. Cows were let out to the fields, and the mare was turned into the croft. The little pigs in the sty were guzzling greedily, squealing and shrieking as they pushed each other aside, and Sam gave one squeal of recognition in their own language.

'We've done for tonight,' said Jimmy. 'Are you coming back with us, or are you going home, Sam?'

'I'm coming with you,' said Sam, and he picked

up his fiddle and hay-rake and followed the Irishmen
back to the shed.

They had supper by the light of candles stuck in the
walls. Sam sat at the trestle table, dangling his feet
from the low form, listening to the merry talk, watching the bats fly across the doorway in the pale moon-
light, and hearing the shrill cries of the swifts which
darted high in the air. The Irishmen told many a tale
of Ireland, and Sam sat nodding his head as they
spoke of their fat little pigs which slept in the cabin
corners and played with the children, and paid the
rent! That was the most astonishing thing of all. To
pay the rent!

But Sam's head rolled sleepily, and Malachi got a
sack of fresh straw and put it in the corner for him.
'Sleep there, little Pigwiggin,' said he. 'Sleep sound,
and then you'll be ready for a good day tomorrow.'

They shut the door to keep him safe and then they
took their sticks and went off to the village. But never
a word did they speak to anyone of their small guest,
for they were true gentlemen. When they returned
Sam was fast asleep. Soon their snores mingled with
his, and the moon looked through the top half of the
door and smiled to herself when she saw Sam in
human company.

The next day Sam was up at dawn to wash in the

stream like the men, and to go out into the fields. The
day passed pleasantly enough for he used his rake, the
little wooden rake that Brock had made for him. Nobody wanted to send him away, although several
people stared at the tiny dwarf who walked so oddly
and raked with such jerky strokes. He was a friend of
the Irishmen's, they said, and as he didn't want any
wages they would ask no questions. His looks were
very peculiar, but looks were not everything, and he
was a good fiddler, and kept the men in a good hu-
mour. Never had the Irishmen been less quarrelsome
than when the little pig was with them.

At last Sam decided to go home. The haymaking
was finished, the last load of hay had been carried by
Sally the mare to the stackyard. The last field had
been raked, and the cattle had been turned into it.
The Irishmen were making their bundles, putting
their clean shirts over their heads, and tying their red
handkerchiefs round their necks.

'Are you coming with us, Sam Pig?' they asked.

'Are you coming with us? Would you like to go
across the sea to dear old Ireland?'

'I couldn't leave Brock and Ann and my brothers,'
said Sam. 'Thank you very much. I must go home.
Brock came to see me last night. He beckoned me
home. He said I'd been away too long, and they all

wanted me. But I have liked working with you.'
Sam spoke proudly and happily to his friends.

'Well, little Pigwiggin,' said Malachi. 'We have decided to give you a pinch of Irish tay, and a wee bottle of our brown cream from our own brown Irish cow. You may like it and you may not. But if ever you meet a fairy, you'll know what to do. Give it a sup.'

The Irishmen whispered together, and laughed and whispered again.

Malachi brought out a basket with a close-shut lid.

'Here! Take this! It's been a trouble to us, and I for one am glad to get rid of it, but it may settle down with you. Here, take it.'

'What is inside?' asked Sam, holding the basket which was very small. 'Is it a kitten?'

'We will leave you to find out,' said Jimmy. 'It followed us from Ireland, and as we're not going back just yet, and as we have had a deal of trouble with it, maybe you'll take it. If you don't want it, then send it packing.'

'Whatever you do, don't open the basket till you get home,' warned Malachi.

'Good-bye and good luck to ye,' they called and they waved their hats to Sam, as he set off. He carried his rake and his fiddle and the little brown basket.

'See you next year. Good luck, Sam Pig.'

'Good luck Malachi and Jimmy and Pat,' squeaked Sam. 'Give my regards to the Pigwiggins of Ireland.'

'Mind the little basket,' called Malachi.

Sam marched across the field. Then he turned round once more to wave. The Irishmen stood looking after him, their round hats on their heads, their blue shirts open, their sun-tanned faces full of smiles. Sam climbed over the gate, and went towards home.

The Leprechaun

When Sam Pig got home from the visit to the Irishmen his brothers and sister ran to welcome him.

'Oh, Sam! How brown you are! As brown as a bear!' they cried hugging him. 'And how did you get on with the Irishmen?'

'Oi've been treated grand,' said Sam, rolling his words in imitation of his friends. 'Oi've been a real Irish haymaker. Och Begorra! Avant there!'

He tossed his battered hat in the corner and put the basket on the table.

'A present from the Irish,' said he. 'And here's a pinch of green tay and a bottle of brown cream from an Irish cow.'

He drew the screwed-up packet and the little bottle from his pocket, and the four pigs crowded round. They pulled out the cork and sniffed and coughed and sneezed.

'They have queer cows in Ireland,' observed Bill. 'It's a strong smell that knocks you over.'

'What is inside the basket, Sam?' asked Ann.

'I don't know. You'd better open it, Ann.'

Ann unlatched the wooden pin and then started back with a cry. Inside, sitting on a bed of hay was a little green-eyed man with a long beard. He wore a leather apron, and a high pointed red hat with an owl's feather. His sleeves were rolled up and he sat cross-legged, hammering a wooden shoe the size of a nutshell.

'Who's this?' asked Ann. 'Who are you?'

The little man sprang from the basket, and stamped and shook his fist. He flung down the hammer and jerked his beard at Ann.

'Who are you?' he squeaked tiny in a shrill voice like the cry of a bit-bat.

'Whatever is it?' whispered the astonished pigs, retreating.

'I'm a Leprechaun, from the land of Ireland, I'd have you know,' said the little man angrily. 'Have you never seen a fairy man before that you stare like that?'

He danced with rage and tapped with his little shoes on the table.

'I thought it was a kitten,' said Sam. 'I thought the Irish had given me a kitten, and it's this – this – fairy man.'

But Badger stepped forward, for the little man

looked so fierce and muttered such queer words the four pigs were alarmed.

'I've heard about you and your tricks and cleverness,' said Brock quietly, pacifying the little creature. 'You are one of the fairy people. You are the fairy shoemaker, with powers of magic. You are one of the ancient people of the earth. I've heard about you from old, old Badgers in the woods. We're an ancient people too. Badgers and Leprechauns were the kings of earth once on a time.'

'Badgers and Leprechauns,' laughed the little man. 'Yes, and the Leprechauns rode on the Badgers.' His fierceness had gone, and he laughed merrily. He swelled with pride when Badger spoke, and he seemed to grow inches taller as he puffed out his chest.

'Yes, I'm a Leprechaun,' said he.

'How did you get here?' asked Brock. 'I know that Sam brought you in this basket, but how was it done?'

'I came from Ireland with the Irish labourers,' said the Leprechaun. 'I wanted to see this country over the sea, where there's never a fairy at all, so they say. It's true, for I've never set eyes on one of the fairy folk all the time I've been here. Not one living creature knows anything of magic.'

The four pigs glanced at Brock, but they said nothing. They remembered how he had changed their cottage to look like a leafy bush with cobwebbed curtains. He knew something of magic, but it was not for them to speak of it.

'The Irishmen didn't like the tricks I played, and they put me in the basket and gave me to Sam Pig. I was willing to come, for I wanted to see what you were like, and maybe I can show you a thing or two.'

'What can you do?' asked Bill. 'Can you cook, or dig the garden, or mend the socks?'

'Hush,' whispered Ann. 'We must be kind to the wee fellow. Don't talk about work, Bill.'

The Leprechaun looked from one to the other with his shrewd green eyes.

'Kind!' he murmured sarcastically, and he snapped his jaws as if he would bite them. 'Kind! Kind to me! I want no kindness! I'm a Leprechaun, I tell ye! I have powers which you know nothing of. I'm a shoemaker.'

'But we don't wear shoes,' said Sam.

'I can see that. You are not men, and that's why I came to visit you. All the same, I shall make my shoes.'

He took a tiny awl from his pocket and pierced the wood. Then he began to tap with his little hammer.

Tap, Tap, Tap, the sound was like a woodpecker. The four pigs stood watching, and suddenly he threw down his work.

'A wooden shoe for the working fairies, those who tread the bogs and lead the traveller astray. A wooden shoe for the fairy who helps the maid in the dairy, and sweeps out the stable for the good stable-boy. A leather shoe for the quality, those who dance and sing before the King. Have you a bit of leather? Bat's-wing for choice?'

Brock reached down a piece of crinkly bat's-wing from his store, and the Leprechaun held it to the light, twisted it between his gnarled fingers, bit it, and looked quickly at Badger.

'This will do. Yes, this will do.' He started to fashion another shoe, with flapping sides and long pointed toe, and he stitched with a bright little needle and cut with a sharp blade of flint.

'Give me a sup of tea,' said he suddenly. 'I've never had a decent drop since I left Ireland.'

The pigs all jumped, they had been so much interested in his shoemaking they had forgotten everything else. Even Sam's home-coming was forgotten in the interest in the fairy man.

Sam ran to the brook to fill the kettle, and he put a pinch of fern and moss in the water to remind the

Leprechaun of Ireland. Bill put a peat on the fire and blew it to make a good flame. He puffed the flames high and sent a breath of smoke into the kettle to flavour the water extra special. Ann poured the boiling water in the old brown teapot. The water was just bubbling with silver beads, and the tea was a bit of the green tea that Sam had brought back from his visit, but Ann had sprinkled in some dried rose-leaves to scent it. Then Badger took the teapot and poured out an egg-cupful. He put a small lump of honey-sugar, and some cream from the cow. Finally he added a lashing of the brown cream from the Irish cow. Then he handed it with ceremony to the Leprechaun, who had been watching with eyes darting with mischief.

The little man sniffed and sniffed at the brew, and his eyes sparkled like coals of fire. He drank the tea, and asked for more, and smacked his lips and rubbed his hands.

'Never have I had such a taste since I left my beloved home in the mountains to come to the fairy-forsaken land,' said he. 'Never have I smelled the good smell of peat and wood-smoke and moss and brown cream and roses, all mingled in a cup of tea.'

He sipped it all up and then he turned back to his work. He wiped his mouth on his leather apron, and stroked his long beard, and cocked his hat awry.

'Anything you like?' he asked.

'What do you mean?' asked Sam.

'I'll give you anything you like for that cup of tea.'

He put his hand in his pocket and threw a fistful of gold on the ground.

'What's the use of that?' asked Ann Pig.

The Leprechaun was surprised at her contempt for gold, so he thought he would try some of his magical tricks on the four pigs. He was full of merriment, eager to show what he could do, and he looked round the room for something to magic.

On the fire was a saucepan brimming with good-smelling nettle broth. In the oven an apple-pie and a rice pudding were cooking.

The Leprechaun stepped over to the hearth. He shook his little apron, and uttered a shrill cry. The saucepan lid rose up, and out of the pan leapt a hare with white fur and little pink nose.

'After it! Catch it!' cried Sam, and they all scampered after the delicate pretty creature. But Badger knew it was only one of the Leprechaun's magics. He spoke a word, and the hare became a bunch of dead-nettle lying on the floor.

'I thought I saw – I thought there was – I thought I saw a white hare,' said Sam, rubbing his eyes.

'How could a hare get into the nettle soup?' asked
Badger calmly, and he tossed the white flowers into
the saucepan and replaced the lid.

The Leprechaun was taken aback by Badger's
knowledge of his charms, but quickly he waved his
little leather apron again. The oven door opened, and
out of the apple-pie flew a white blackbird. It piped

and fluttered round the room. It whistled a wild song, and flashed its gleaming wings.

'Catch it! After it! A white blackbird,' cried Sam. Ann threw her duster after it, Bill and Tom chased it with their hats. But Badger saw it was not real, it was only another bit of the Leprechaun's magic. He gave a soft call and the blackbird became an apple which had fallen out of the pie.

'I thought – I thought – I thought I saw a white blackbird come out of the pie,' said Sam, rubbing his eyes.

'How could a blackbird come out of an apple-pie?' asked Brock, and he raised the pie-crust and returned the apple to its place.

Then the Leprechaun tried another trick. He looked round the room and there was Sam's fiddle hanging from a hook in the ceiling. He waved his little apron and out of the fiddle came a stream of white butterflies, hundreds of them, floating down with their soft wings beating and their tiny eyes aglow.

Sam cried out and stretched up his hands. 'White butterflies in my fiddle!' he exclaimed. Ann sprang after them and Bill and Tom tried to hold them. Like water they slipped from their grasp. But Badger knew that this was another of the magics of the Leprechaun.

They were not real butterflies but dream melodies unplayed but imagined.

He gave a soft alluring whistle and the butterflies disappeared like mist. Out of the fiddle came the most beautiful music, and the tunes floated down like the Leprechaun's butterflies.

'I thought – I thought – I thought I saw some white butterflies coming from my fiddle,' said Sam, staring up at it.

'How could butterflies come from your fiddle, Sam?' asked Brock. 'There are only tunes inside.'

He lifted it down and shook it, and the strings stopped vibrating, the delicate airs were stilled.

Then the Leprechaun knew that he was beaten at his own game. He had met his match in Badger. So he took off his little red hat, and bowed low to the famous old Brock.

'Where did you learn your magic, sir?' he asked. 'We were told that this was the land where all the old rites were forgotten, and the fairies were dead.'

'Some of us remember,' said Badger. 'Some of us have long memories. Our grandfathers have told us, and their grandfathers told them. Back to the ancient days when fairies lived in the woods our memories go.'

'Ah!' cried the Leprechaun. 'Then I don't think

I am wanted in this country. There is nothing I can teach you. I'll be getting back to Ireland.'

'Oh, stay with us,' cried Sam. 'Don't go away yet, Mister. We want to see a few more of your magical tricks. Don't leave us.'

'Yes, stay with us,' added the Badger persuasively, and he held out his paw in friendship. 'The Irishmen are working at another farm, and I will take you to them when they go back to Ireland. Wait here a wee while and make your shoes in comfort. There are a few elves about in hidden places, but there is no shoe-maker. They'll be glad of a pair of Irish shoes for their little bare feet when they dance in the fairy rings. Do stay with us.'

'And we'll make you a little bed in the corner of the hearth,' said Ann.

'And we'll put a heather mattress for you,' said Sam.

'And a pillow of wild thyme,' said Tom.

'And a blanket of wool from the black sheep,' said Bill.

'And we'll feed you on honey-comb and heather ale, and herb cheeses,' said Ann.

'And you shall have as much bat's-wing leather as you like,' said Brock.

'And a blue jay's feather for your hat,' said Sam.

So the Leprechaun agreed to stop for a few days, to share the home of the four pigs and Brock the Badger. What happened I cannot tell you for it would fill a book to speak of half the magics which the Leprechaun worked. Badger was busy straightening them out from morning till night, and through the night too, when the Leprechaun was particularly frolicsome.

Swallows flew out of the teapot, and roses blossomed in the saucepans. The toasting fork became a fiery serpent, and the rolling-pin a bowl of goldfish. Bees hummed in the kettle and nightingales sang in Ann's work-basket. Even Ann herself was changed for one dazzling minute into a green woodpecker, and Sam became a little grey donkey which brayed and kicked and stamped about the garden.

It was all very exciting, but it was tiring, for nobody knew what would happen next. The chairs danced together, the table spun on one leg, and the beds shut up like mousetraps with the little pigs inside. The Leprechaun nearly split his sides with laughter, and Brock worked very hard upsetting the little man's tricks.

Sometimes, of course, it was very pleasant, as when the Leprechaun produced a hammock from a spider's web and gave them all swings, and again when he fitted wings on their shoulders so that they could flit across the garden and perch uneasily in the trees. Badger didn't approve of such flights, and he soon brought them back to earth. He didn't want his little friends to get stuck at the top of the oak-tree, or lost in the clouds. So although they enjoyed the visit of the Leprechaun, the four pigs were secretly relieved when he said he must be going.

'Then I'll take you part of the way,' said Badger. 'You might get lost in one of the big towns, and you'd never get out with all the magic in the world.'

It was agreed that Brock should take the fairy fellow in his pocket for safety, and off they went that very same night. They travelled the woods and lanes of England, going quickly in the darkness, resting by day, using their magic when danger was near. At last they reached Liverpool, where the cargo boat was waiting. Up the gangway went three large men, with bundles on their backs and thick cudgels in their brown hands.

'The Irish,' cried the Leprechaun, peeping from Brock's pocket. 'There they are, bless them! There's the three of them, Pat and Jimmy and Malachi. I shall be safe with them.'

So Brock put the tiny fellow down and bade him good-bye.

'Good-bye, Leprechaun, and good luck to you, who are luck itself.'

'Good-bye, Badger,' said the Leprechaun. 'Don't forget that magic I taught you about moonshine. It might come in useful some day.'

'And don't forget that bit of magic about the brown cream,' said Badger laughing. 'I've got the little bottle here for you to take back to Ireland, for the pigs don't like it.'

'Ah!' said the Leprechaun. 'Thank you. Your house is the nicest place on this side of the water, and yours is the best family, Brock.'

Then the Leprechaun ran up the gangway, slipping under a sailor's arm, skipping past the captain like a flash of light. He caught hold of an Irishman's coat tail, and Brock saw Malachi stoop down and pick him up and put him in his bundle. The boat began to move, and Brock stood on the quay, a small squat rough little person, looking up at the vessel. The Irishmen waved to their friends ashore, and the Badger waved to his friend on board. But the little Leprechaun took a tiny shoe, all worked with gold thread and stitched with the smallest stitches ever seen. He tossed the tiny object across the water, high in the air, and it alighted in Brock's paw. The Badger closed his fist over it and put it in his pocket.

When he got home he placed it on the mantelpiece, next to his money-box and clock.

Sometimes the four pigs sat on the doorstep watching the stars and the moon and the glowing pageant of heaven, and then Brock got down the little fairy shoe. He held it in his paw and told them stories of the magics that the Leprechaun could do, for the shoe had the power of its master, and Badger knew many strange things when he touched its gilded leather.

The Theatre

'Have you ever been to a theatre, Badger?' asked Sam Pig one day when the little family sat at dinner.

What a strange question to ask! Bill Pig stopped with a roast potato half-way to his mouth, and Tom Pig dropped his bread on the floor. Ann opened wide her small blue eyes and gasped with astonishment. What was brother Sam talking about now! Only Brock the Badger took it calmly. Not one of his black-and-silver hairs quivered, not a muscle moved. He took up a piece of toast and dripping and had a bite before he answered the young pig.

'No,' he drawled. 'I can't say as I've ever been to a theatre, Sam.'

'But what is it? What is a theatre?' they all asked quickly.

'It's a play-acting house, where everyone pretends to be somebody else,' explained Sam proud of his knowledge.

'Like the Wolf pretending to be a poor lone sheep?' asked Ann. 'I shouldn't like that at all.'

'Like the Fox pretending to be dead?' asked Bill.

'Like a falling leaf pretending to be a butterfly?' asked Tom.

'Well, something like those things,' said Sam. 'I've never actually been to a theatre, but I've been talking to Sally the mare, and she says there's a theatre on Midsummer Eve.'

'Where? Oh where?' they asked in a gabble of surprise.

'At the farm, in the stable or barn, I don't know exactly. We are all invited, and they asked me to take my fiddle,' said Sam.

'It's Midsummer Eve tomorrow,' said Badger. 'Well, I've never seen a theatre, so we will all go together, and see the fun, whatever it is.'

There were great preparations. Sam Pig had a bath in the wash-tub the night before, and on the morning of Midsummer Eve he scrubbed his face so that it shone like a lamp.

'If there wasn't a moon we could see by the light of your face,' said Bill.

Then Sam threw a clod of soil at Bill, and Bill tossed it back again, and Sam had to wash once more.

Tom got out his blacking-pot and the brushes and he polished everybody's hooves. Ann gave a twist and curl to all the little tails and she swept a little furze

brush over the creamy hairs on her brother's heads.
Badger was very busy in his bedroom, making himself into a fine country gentleman. Bill brought but-
ton-holes of moss roses and parsley for each of the
pigs to wear. Tom gave out sticks of barley honey for
each of them to suck. Barley honey is made out of
honey-comb and ground barley, and very delicious it
is.

Badger cut stout staffs to help them on the journey, and Sam as usual got in everybody's way as he ran here and there trying to help.

At last it was time to depart. The moon had risen and the stars were peeping through the soft clouds. A little breeze ruffled the leaves and the woods sang their evening hymn to the coming of night. The fields were silvery with dew, and a nightingale sang in the oak-tree.

'Jug. Jug. Jug. Tirra la-a-a. How happy I am! Sweet. Sweet,' it sang and they all stood listening to its exquisite voice.

'We're going to a theatre. Tirra la-a-a,' piped Sam in his thinnest wee voice, as he tried to rival the bird.

'How happy I am! I have a mate and a nest with a brood of young ones,' sang the bird in rapture.

'Be quiet, Sam,' chided Brock. 'Animals are silent when they walk the woods by night. Only the nightingale and the owl may raise their voices. Come along softly and don't walk in the moon shadows, or the goblins will get you. They'll pull your tail and swing you on their backs and carry you off.'

Sam looked quickly behind him at the blue shadows. Then he saw that Badger was laughing at him, so he pressed close to his friend and trotted quietly along.

When they arrived at the farm they tiptoed very
gently over the lawn and round the flower-beds, for it
would never do to leave a trail on the soil. The watchdog lay in his kennel with one eye watching them. He
gave no alarm, for of course he knew about the festivi-
ties. The farmhouse was in darkness with the shutters

closed and never a glimmer of light showing. On Midsummer Eve it was considered dangerous to be abroad, for strange things happened.

The animals padded across the yard to the stable from which came a faint glow. They pushed their way through the little crowd in the doorway and gazed around in admiration.

The horses' stalls were festooned with green leaves, and from the roof hung a horn lantern with a light like a pale moon. The mangers were filled with forget-me-nots and the walls were decked with streamers of ivy. In the wall-holes where usually the horse-brushes and currycombs were kept, there stood hollowed turnips with candles burning within. A multitude of glow-worms lay among the flowers and leaves on the walls, and gave out their clear green light, tiny and fairy.

One part of the stable was screened off with a leafy curtain and from behind it came muffled laughter, high squeals, and subdued whispers. The curtain scarcely reached the ground and Sam Pig could see little black feet jumping up and down behind it.

The horses were in the stalls, and these were the best seats of all, for of course it was their theatre. Although their backs were to the stage their long heads were turned and their brown eyes gazed in mild surprise. On the partitions of the stalls, perched on the curving oak ledges, were red and white hens, and a couple of cocks splendid in burnished feathers and glittering spurs. They were in the gallery. They were noisy creatures and never ceased pushing and chattering, crowing and cackling even in the most pathetic moment when the heroine lost her slipper.

The body of the stable was occupied by Sally the mare, by the farm pigs, the young calves, and a dozen or more sheep and lambs. The sheep were huddled together looking rather frightened, but the sheep-dog reassured them.

'It's only pretence,' said he, and everybody told everyone else. 'It's only pretence.'

Badger modestly led the way to the back of the stable but the farmyard animals gave up their seats at the front. The door was closed, so that even the moon could not look at the curious scene. Somebody blew out the lamp in the roof, and then the stable was lighted only by the turnip candles and the glow-worms, but a faint gleam came from behind that magical curtain of leaves upon which all eyes were fixed.

The Alderney cow shook her head so that her bell tinkled. Sally the mare twitched the curtain aside, and nibbled a few leaves in her excitement. Everybody cried 'Oh-o-o-o-o-o-o!'

There were the seven little pigs from the pig-cote, dressed as fairies, in pink skirts with wreaths of rosebuds round their pink ears. They danced on their nimble black toes, and swung their ballet skirts. They pirouetted until the hens cried out to them.

'Stop a minute! It makes us giddy to watch you!'

'Hush,' said Badger indignantly. 'Hush! No talking!' and the hens stopped clucking for a whole minute and stared down at Badger's black-and-white head.

A band of music makers played in a corner. There was a lamb with a shepherd's pipe, and a Scottish terrier with bagpipes and a kitten with a drum.

'Come along, Sam, and join us,' they beckoned, and Sam stepped shyly through the little dancing pigs who never stopped whirling. He tuned his fiddle and sat down in the corner. Soon he was sawing with might and main, trying to keep time with the squealing of the Scottie's bagpipes, the fluting of the lamb's pipe and the drumming of the little cat.

The farmyard pigs sang their own shrill songs, and the audience joined in the choruses of 'John Barleycorn' and 'A Frog he would a-wooing go'.

They gave an acrobatic display and leaped

through hoops of leafy willow on to Sally's broad back. They bowed and bowed again and then the curtain was drawn. It was the interval.

The mother of the dancing pigs handed round refreshments, elderberry wine, and cowslip ale, and cakes of herbs and bunches of hay.

They were all eating and drinking when the Alderney rang her bell. The mare twitched the curtain back, and the lantern went out. Quickly they stuffed their cakes in their mouths and hid their drinking-mugs in the ivy. There was now to be acted the famous play of Cinderella and her straw slipper.

The smallest pig sat in rags by the empty fireplace, and the fine sisters went off to the ball, flaunting their long skirts and their pheasant feathers.

In came a pair of rats drawing a pumpkin across the stable floor. There was such a rustle and flutter among the cocks who wanted to fly down and attack them, such a hiss from the cat, and such a growl from the Scottie, Badger had to stand up and quieten them.

'It's all pretence,' said he, and they echoed 'Pretence,' and were quiet.

The Fairy Godmother waved her wand, and Cinderella's rags fell off. Behold! She was a pink-skirted pigling! Away she went to the ball, riding on the pumpkin, trundling herself along the floor with her little hooves which were covered with shoes of yellow straw.

The next scene was the ballroom, where everyone in the stable danced. Badger danced the polka with the Scottie, and Ann Pig turned with a lamb. Little Sam Pig was chosen by Cinderella herself and he was in great confusion as he tripped and skipped and stumbled over her straw slippers. But the stable clock struck twelve, and Cinderella ran away. Sam tried to hold her but she escaped and hid in a corner out of sight. One of the slippers lay on the floor. Sam Pig picked it up and put it in his pocket.

'Sam Pig! Sam Pig!' called the sow. 'You must go round the theatre and see whose foot is small enough to fit into the little straw slipper.'

'But I know!' answered Sam quickly. 'It belongs to the little Cinderella pig.'

'Hist! Do what I tell you! This is a theatre and it's all pretence,' said the sow sternly. So Sam walked round with the little straw slipper, and everybody tried it on. The mare held out her great hoof, the Alderney held up her delicate foot. The sheep held up their little hooves, and the hens clucked and fussed and stretched out their long thin toes. Little Ann Pig

got the slipper on and tried to keep it, but Sam refused to give it up.

'It's not yours, Ann,' he whispered crossly.

Even Badger held out his hairy pad, but Sam pushed it aside.

'I told you so! I told you so! It isn't yours and you can't have it. It belongs to that nice little Cinderella pig, and I don't know where she is.'

He pushed the ugly sisters aside, and there, hiding among the besoms and harness and horse-rugs was little Cinderella. She held out a neat little hoof and Sam Pig dragged the straw slipper upon it. It fitted like a glove!

'Hurrah!' they all cried. 'The Princess is found.' As for Sam he was so excited he leaned towards her and gave her a kiss. You remember the old woman in the wood who kissed him? Sam never forgot that nice feeling. Now he kissed Cinderella.

'Hurrah!' cried everybody. 'Hurrah! The Prince has kissed Cinderella.'

'But it's all pretence,' they told one another.

The stable-door flew open, and they all flocked out into the cool night air. The sheep scampered away to the pasture, the Alderney walked sedately to the field. The pigs hastened to the pig-cote and nestled together in the shelter of their little home. The cocks and hens scurried back to the hen-place, escorted by the Scottie. The Fox was staring over the wall, wondering what was happening that midsummer night, but he turned aside when he saw Hamish the Scottie. The cat came out last, and she climbed up on the stable roof.

Brock and the four pigs trundled over the fields to their little home, chattering softly of all they had seen.

'So that's a theatre!' said Brock. 'It was grand! And you, Sam Pig, were the Prince!'

Sam said nothing. All his thoughts were on the little pigling called Cinderella whom he had kissed by the light of the turnip lanterns.

'But it's all pretence,' murmured Ann, and the others echoed, 'Yes. All pretence.'

The Flower Show

Sam Pig went out walking one day with Bill and Tom and little Ann. They were going to meet Badger.

'At the corner of Forty-acre field,' Brock had said when he left home the day before. 'I will wait for you at the corner.'

Now Forty-acre was the name given to a tiny little croft, no bigger than a cottage garden. The field was so small it was called Forty-acre in joke. But the four pigs did not know this, and they started off to find a very large field, where they expected to see Brock waiting for them. Sam was quite sure he knew which was the field, and he said he would take the others there. It was the largest field he had ever seen.

He led the way along the lanes, and across the meadows, through a beautiful field where he had watched the lambs at play in the spring. The lambs were now sheep and they came up to Sam when he asked them if they had seen Brock passing that way. They were going to meet him at Forty-acre field.

'Forty-acre?' they said. 'That must be the large

field across the road. It is famous for its size, and its smooth grass. We went there for a few weeks to graze, but we were turned out and sent here again. There's a Flower Show or something on today, and they don't want sheep.'

In the distance the four pigs could hear the faint sound of a drum beating and a trumpet playing. Among the trees they could see white tents and little flags waving.

'That must be the field Badger meant,' said they. 'Thank you very much. Badger will be there, for he likes flowers.'

'If I were you I should take a few flowers with you,' advised one of the sheep. 'It seems the right thing to do when you go to a Flower Show. There's plenty of blossoms and berries in this meadow of ours. Take a bunch with you.'

'Yes, do,' said another sheep. 'I've seen people going along the road, and every one of them took some flowers.'

'Our missis, the farmer's wife, was picking roses last night, and the farmer was taking the marrows to the Show,' said a third sheep. 'It's the right and proper thing to do.'

'There's harebells in quantities, and pretty orchis, and many a flower in this field,' said the first sheep.

'We don't eat them, for we don't like the taste, but you'll find some beauties if you look about.'

So the four pigs ran about in the grass, and gathered fine bunches of flowers from under the great hedge and by the hollows of the stream. They thought they had never seen so many lovely flowers before. They sat down by the water and Ann arranged them into one large bunch with little sprays of green ferns and beaded grasses dropping like fountains over them, and clusters of bright berries among them.

'It's like a bridal bouquet,' said Sam. 'I saw a wedding when I was with Man, and the bride carried a bunch like that, but not so pretty.'

The others were much impressed by Sam's information. Ann felt very proud and walked ahead of the others, with the great bunch of many-coloured flowers held high, so that she could hardly see where she was going. Tall purple thistles pricked her nose, long foxgloves tickled her ears, and the scabious and bed-straw and bell-flowers sent their lovely spikes drooping nearly to her shoulders.

'Do you think it will be quite safe to go to a Flower Show?' asked Bill, hesitating, as a pony and trap rushed past. 'Do you think they will stop us? Will it be all right?'

'Why not? What harm could happen to us?

Didn't we once go to a Fair? A Flower Show is
nothing much. Only flowers. And Badger will be
waiting for us somewhere in one of the corners of the
field.'

'This is Forty-acre sure enough,' said Tom. 'Look
at the size of it. Look at the hedge going on and on,

and the great green field, as big as the wood where we live.'

'Listen to the music,' cried Sam, excitedly, and he gave a little skip and a jump. 'Listen. There's a flute going tootle-too, and a drum going bang! bang! bang! and a trumpet playing. Oh, how I wish I had my fiddle with me! That's a fine rousing tune. I must remember it. Tum-tiddly tum-tum. Tum-ti-tum.'

He marched in time to the music of the band, and the others kept step with him. They came to the great white gate which led to the field, and there stood a man with a money-box and a pile of shillings on a small table. Ann walked boldly on, never hesitating, with the bouquet held up before her face.

'Children with exhibits free,' said the gate-keeper. 'Are you all together? Oh, yes.' The others shuffled quickly up to Ann.

'You must be quick or you'll be too late with those flowers,' said the man kindly. 'Hurry up, little 'uns, and go into that tent to the right over there. They'll be judging in a minute or two.'

He pointed to a large tent with a blue flag waving on it, and then he turned to the next comers.

Sam gave a sigh of relief. 'Well! That was easy! I didn't think there would be somebody to guard the Show. I've never got into a place like this before.'

They trotted across the grass to the white tent with its open doorway. They stopped for a moment at the entrance, to sniff at the delicious scent of vegetables which came to their quivering noses. It was heavenly! Then timidly they stepped into the shaded canvas-walled room, whispering, nudging one another, staring with their little bright eyes at the beautiful sight. Above their heads flapped the white roof of the tent, and under their feet was soft grass. All round the walls of the tent were vegetables and flowers displayed in all their loveliness on well-scrubbed tables.

Never had they seen so many dinners spread out and nobody eating them! There was a dinner of potatoes, scrubbed clean and ready for the oven, pink-eyed and oval. There was a dinner of green peas, and French beans, arranged evenly on dishes, and decked with bunches of parsley. There were long straight cucumbers, and enormous marrows as big as Sam Pig himself. As for the crimson apples, and the yellow pears, and the bunches of bloomy grapes, the little pigs fairly squealed with delight. Massed tables of flowers came next, but the little pigs scarcely looked at the roses, the blue delphiniums, and the silver lilies, they were too enraptured with the ripe sweet fruits spread out there.

'Here! Come along! You're just in time,' called a

voice, and a man hurried them away from the tables where they stood. At the end of the tent was a bench where bunches of wild flowers were set out in jam-pots and bowls. They were little country nosegays gathered by the village children and stuffed into the pots.

'Give me your bunch, little girl,' said a lady. 'It *is* a pretty bouquet. You were nearly too late.'

The other ladies gave little cries of admiration as they looked at Ann's flowers.

'So original,' they whispered. 'So clever and modern, with those tall stiff spikes and those droop-ing grasses.'

'What's your name?' they asked, stooping over little Ann.

She hung her head, for she wasn't sure what they were saying. The only one who really understood Man's language was Sam, and he spoke up.

'Ann Pig,' said he in a loud squeak.

'Oh, Ann Pig? Well, we'll put it here, in this jam-pot, and in a minute or two it will be judged.'

'What extraordinary children!' whispered the lady.

'They know where the wild flowers grow,' laughed her companion. 'Perhaps they are gipsy children. I never saw such a beautiful bunch. The way those grasses and berries are mingled is a lesson to many of us.'

'They certainly deserve the first prize,' said the judge, putting on his spectacles and leaning close to look at them.

He took a red card from his pocket and stuck it in front of Ann's flowers.

'First Prize,' it said. 'Awarded to Ann Pig for a bunch of wild flowers.'

The four little pigs were already walking away up the tent, stopping here and there to take a sniff at white celery and flaming tomatoes.

'Are they to eat? Can we have some?' asked Ann.

'I'm hungry,' said Tom. 'We didn't bring any sandwiches, Ann, and I've had nothing to eat since breakfast. There's all these dinners ready.'

'I want some of those round lettuces. Look at them. They are bigger than those Brock grows. And look at the radishes! Oh!'

But Sam wasn't sure. Memories of Man remained with him, of shops full of food, where nobody could help themselves, of meals prepared, and nothing given away. He looked round and saw eyes watching, and people turning to stare after four odd little folk who trotted along on short legs chattering softly with grunts and squeaks and strange rumbling laughter.

'Not yet,' he whispered. 'Let's get out of this and see the band. I want to see the big drum.'

'They took my flowers,' pouted Ann. 'I think we ought to have at least a cabbage.'

She stretched out her hand, but somebody stepped forward.

'Now then! No touching the exhibits, please, Miss.' Sam hurried her away.

'We've got to find Badger,' he reminded her.

But there was another tent next door and they couldn't resist the homely smells. There were baskets of brown eggs, and tables of great round cheeses as big as wheels. There were tight square honey-combs, not roughly shaped like those Sam found in his honey-trees, and shells of beeswax. The four pigs sighed with rapture and snuffled the fragrant air. Fathers and mothers and little children were walking round and the four pigs followed after, keeping in the shadow of the women's skirts, pressing close to the children.

It was much easier to admire without being noticed in this tent, and Ann shot out her pink tongue and gave a passing lick to many a pat of butter and honey-comb.

When they got out of the tent each pig carried something. Ann had a small country cheese tucked

under her arm, and Sam had a pot of honey. Bill had
a few eggs and Tom a pat of butter and a cob of
bread. They looked at each other and laughed. Then
they hurried to the corner of the field and sat down to
eat their food. They divided the bread and cheese and
sucked the eggs from their shells.

'This is what I call a good Flower Show, for there's
more than flowers. Flowers don't fill the stomach like
cheese and eggs,' said Bill.

'And there's plenty to eat in that first tent,' Sam
reminded him. 'We will go back soon when the
people come out.'

'There's no sign of Badger in this corner,' said
Ann. 'I don't believe he is here at all.'

'Oh, he will find us. Clever Brock won't desert us!
He will walk round till he finds us,' Tom assured
her.

They finished their food and watched the company
of red-coated bandsmen with their brass instruments.
There was a round drum, and a long trumpet, and a
cornet, as well as other strange things which shot in
and out and made loud noises. The bandsmen went
away for refreshments, and left their instruments on
the grass. Sam Pig crept up and beat the drum,
tum-tum-tum, very softly. He tried to play the cornet
and the trumpet, but although he blew till his cheeks

were like balloons he couldn't get any sound from
them. Then Ann tried to blow, and Bill and Tom.
The men were eating their tea in the tent, and nobody noticed the small pigs hovering in the shade of
the trees.

'It's no good,' said Sam. 'Only Man can play
these things. They have more breath than we. But I
can play the drum. Listen!'

He climbed on top of the drum and gave a hard
thump with the drumstick. At the same time he
banged with his sharp heels. There was a loud report,
and into the drum fell Sam.

The men came running from the tent when they
heard the noise, and Sam scrambled out of the hole
and scampered after Ann and his brothers. He was
terribly frightened, and squealed as he ran.

'It's those children meddling,' shouted the bandsmen angrily. 'Never can leave things alone! Be off
with you! Be off! I saw them sitting watching us,
looking so innocent, and look what they've done!'

But Sam and Bill and Tom and Ann were running
along the hedge as fast as they could scamper. They
scuttled through a hole and ran into the next field.

'Oh dear! Never try to play a drum,' panted Sam.
'I nearly got stuck fast inside it. Who would have
thought it was hollow?'

'All drums are hollow,' said a deep voice, and Sam started back. There was Badger, half-hidden in the earth, watching them.

'Oh Brock, Brock!' they all cried, clinging to him. 'Where have you come from? We've been looking for you everywhere.'

'And I've been looking for you, silly billies. Didn't I say the Forty-acre field, and here you are at a Flower Show.'

'But isn't this Forty-acre?' they asked.

'No. This is the Home Park. Forty-acre is that little croft near home where the cowslips grow in spring. It's only half an acre really – the name's a joke.'

'Well, we had a feast,' said Sam. 'Honey and bread and butter and cheese.'

'And our flowers are stuck in a jam-pot in the tent.'

'And we've listened to the brass band.'

'And I fell into the drum.'

'How did you find us?'

'When you didn't come I walked about and saw your tracks. They were quite easy to see, little hoof-marks cut in the grass. I followed you, and when I heard the band I guessed you had gone to the Show. I was afraid something might happen to you there. How did you get in? They wouldn't let me go through the gate.'

'Oh Brock, we carried a bunch of flowers, and they welcomed us! They said the bunch was pretty enough for the first prize, and we left it behind.'

'If you had all those good things to eat it seems to me you helped yourselves to a few first prizes,' said Badger drily. 'Now come along home. You won't want any supper tonight, but remember *I* am hungry. I've not been to a Flower Show. I've had no prize.'

So the little pigs trotted home with Badger, and all the way they chattered of what they had seen. Cheeses as big as the moon, eggs as brown as the ploughfields, cucumbers like tree trunks, marrows like fat piglings, cabbages like footstools. The Flower Show was a magical place, where everything grew to a giant's size.

'It would just have suited the Dragon,' said Brock. 'It's a pity he didn't go there with you.'

'He might have eaten the bandsmen,' said Sam, 'and that would have been a pity. I would like to be a bandsman some day when I grow up, Brock. Then I can play the drum.'

'We'll see,' said Brock kindly and he took Sam's fist and squeezed it in his big paws.

At the Flower Show a lady was calling Ann Pig's name.

'First prize for the best bunch of wild flowers is

awarded to Ann Pig. I should like to say that never in my life have I seen such a tasteful bunch, with colours so happily mingled. Come forward, Ann Pig, and take your prize. Ann Pig! Ann Pig!'

Everyone clapped heartily and everyone looked round for Ann Pig.

'Ann Pig! Ann Pig!' they called, but nobody came forward. The prize is waiting yet.

The Snow Goose

Winter was coming and the wind tore the leaves from the trees and threw them down to the ground in showers.

'The wind's in a frolic today. He's stripping the trees and the poor things will be cold,' remarked Ann Pig. She took her little birch-besom to sweep up the leaves, but they lay so thick in the woods she had to let the wind have his own way.

Then wild gales raged from the north, and the trees were rocked and shaken.

'Let us gather firewood for the winter,' said Ann, and they all ran out to collect the fallen branches, to store in the wood-shed.

Next came snow, and the soft flakes fell like feathers fluttering from the heavy clouds.

'The Old Grey Woman is plucking the white geese up yonder,' said Ann, pointing to the sky. She shivered and went indoors to the fireside, but Sam Pig stood looking up, trying to see the great white birds whose feathers were falling so fast they covered the fields and woods. It was very cold and the wind cut his cheeks like a knife, so he followed Ann and sat with his brothers in the warm kitchen.

No outside work could be done. The stream was frozen, and Bill had to break a hole in the ice with a stone to fill the kettle. There was plenty to eat, and

the snow didn't matter, for it was very cosy in the house of the four pigs. There were strings of onions hanging in ropes from the beams of the ceiling, and a heap of carrots under straw in the larder. The wood-shed was piled with potatoes and logs of wood to roast them. Tom Pig made good warm soup every day, and Sam shook the pepper pot over it. It was as hot as a fire, and it kept their innards comfortable.

Away in the Fox's house it was dismal and cold, for Mister Fox hadn't had a good meal for weeks, not since the little wicker boat was sunk. He had been out every night to the rabbit warren, but the rabbits kept close to their homes and wrapped themselves in fur blankets and curled up in bed to keep warm. The Fox kept watch on the pond where the water-hens and ducks lived, but the water was frozen and the birds were wary. They saw the tracks of the Fox in the snow, and they hid themselves. Then the Fox went to the farm, hoping to catch a hen for supper. The dog was loose and he frightened the Fox away.

So the Fox got very thin with hunger, and when he met fat little Sam Pig, who had just eaten a plateful of hot vegetable soup, he was really angry. Sam Pig was going to make a slide, but he stopped when he saw the Fox.

'Have you seen any geese about?' asked the Fox with a sneer.

Sam opened wide his little blue eyes. 'Geese? No,' said he.

'I thought you might know of a few ganders as you know everything,' scoffed the Fox, hungrily.

'The Old Grey Woman is plucking the white geese up in the sky,' said Sam, catching a snowflake and eating it.

'How do you know that?' asked the Fox with a sharp bark.

'Here are the feathers,' said Sam, innocently. 'Look at them. There's a big flock of geese up there in the fields of the sky, and the Woman is plucking the feathers off and throwing them down to the earth. Ann says so, and it must be true.'

The Fox was impressed.

'I could do with one of those fat geese,' said he. 'Where do you think they live, Sam Pig?'

'In the sky somewhere,' said Sam, hesitating and looking up. 'There's maybe great fields up there, and ponds and streams where the geese can swim. That's what the rain is, I 'specks. It's a pond running over and coming down on us.'

'Yes,' said the Fox. 'That's it.'

'I don't know how you will catch a goose from up

there,' said Sam, and he ate a few feathers thought-
fully. 'Not unless the Old Grey Woman lets one slip
from her knees.'

'I wish she would,' said the Fox fervently.

'They'll be cold if they are like this feather,' said
Sam, shivering.

'I don't care if they are cold as ice as long as I can
get my teeth into them,' said the Fox. 'When they are
alive they are warm. It's because the feathers have
dropped such a long way on a winter's morning that
they are so cold.'

Sam agreed that it might be so.

'I will wait here till a goose falls from the Old Grey
Woman's knee,' said the Fox, and he sat down in the
snow with his head raised to the sky, waiting.

Sam didn't bother to make his slide. He went
home to ask all about snow geese.

When he told his brothers that the Fox was waiting
for a snow goose to drop from the sky they laughed.

'Let's make one for him,' they said. 'It would be a
pity if he waited for nothing, poor old Fox.'

They ran to the back of the house and worked
quickly, with handfuls of snow. They made a
beautiful snow goose. It had a large smooth body, and
a long neck and a neat head. They fixed a pair of
feathery wings, ruffled and cut from the snow. Then

Sam put a pair of little shiny pebbles for the eyes, and they all stood back to admire their work.

'Did you ever see such a big goose?' they whispered. 'It is much more fun than making a snow pig, or even a snow man. A snow goose is a fine bird, and this is as real as life.'

Sam carried it out to the field and placed it under a tree. Then he ran off to find the Fox, who was still waiting.

'Mister Fox! There's a snow goose under yonder tree. He must have flown down from the sky. Come quickly before he goes off. Oh, he is such a big one!'

The Fox shook the snow from his back and ran after Sam Pig.

'What a beautiful goose!' he cried. 'Thank you, Sam Pig. It will feed us all. Thank you.'

He hauled the goose on to his back and walked away. The goose was very large and the Fox was nearly covered with the snowy body. As he went through the woods the heat of his fur began to melt the snow goose, and the weight of it pressed upon him. The water turned to ice again, and stuck to his back.

'Whatever have you got there?' asked his wife as he staggered in at the door.

'A snow goose, fallen from the sky,' said the Fox

triumphantly. 'Come, wife, and take it off my back, for it seems to have frozen on me.'

So she pulled and pulled and the Fox shook himself and at last the snow goose fell to the ground.

'Why, it's only a heap of snow,' cried Mrs Fox. 'How foolish you are, Reynard.'

'It's a snow goose from the sky, one of the geese which drop their feathers when it snows, my dear,' the Fox assured her, and he pulled the goose to pieces. 'Sam Pig helped me to catch it,' he added.

'You are a snow goose yourself,' snapped Mrs Fox. 'Young Sam Pig has tricked you again.'

'You are right as usual,' said the Fox ruefully, looking up from the snowy heap. They both vowed vengeance on little Sam Pig as they watched the wings and the long smooth neck and the stiff little legs fall to the floor and run away like water.

Now a few days later Sam was coming back from the hen-place with a few eggs he had collected. Eggs are scarce in cold weather, and the hens had not been laying. Brother Bill fed them on warm scraps and they were so pleased they decided to give him some eggs. They clucked loudly to tell Sam all about it, and he ran through the snow calling back to them.

'Sam Pig, Sam Pig. We've laid some eggs,' they shouted in their clucking voices, and Sam Pig answered, 'Thank you. Thank you, dear Fluff and Bluff, and Snow-white and Rose-red and the rest of you.'

He gathered the eggs from the warm nests, patted the hen's soft feathers, and started back home. But to his surprise he saw the Fox waiting for him. At first Sam was rather frightened, remembering the snow goose, but the Fox came smiling up to him and held out a paw.

'Shake, Sam Pig! Shake!' cried the Fox. 'I want to thank you, Sam Pig. You saved me from starvation, Sam. Shake a paw!'

Sam put down the basket and held out his little fist, and the Fox shook it up and down so hard that Sam was nearly thrown off his balance. Perhaps the Fox didn't know how much it hurt, for he kept smiling, so Sam smiled back, although it was only a little wry smile he gave the Fox.

'You remember that snow goose you found, Sam Pig,' said the Fox, and Sam, trembling a little, said that he remembered.

'It was a wonderful goose, so fat, so luscious, so tender that it melted in my mouth,' said the Fox.

Sam listened, uneasily.

'Yes, Sam Pig, I shall always be grateful to you for your kindness in telling me of the geese which the Old

Grey Woman is plucking up in the sky, and for giving me such a fat one.'

Sam's eyes widened. He could scarcely believe his ears.

'And that was not the end,' continued the Fox, 'for the next day I found another snow goose, and this one was alive. It had flown down from the sky and there it was a-sitting in the wood as tame as a hen.'

'Oh my!' cried Sam Pig. 'I wish I had seen it.'

'It's in my wood-shed,' said the Fox. 'It's so tame I haven't the heart to eat it. Besides, it is laying eggs for me. Each day it lays two dozen eggs. You never saw anything like them for size. As for flavour! And shape! And goodness! Words can't tell their excellence.'

The Fox spoke slowly and Sam's eyes were popping out of his head. His breath came panting in excitement, and his red tongue licked his lips. Marvels would never cease!

The Fox continued, 'Those eggs are the best-tasting I ever had, with yolks all rich and whites as pure as the driven snow. We poach them, and scramble them, and make omelettes with them, and boil them, but we can't use them all up. Think of it! Two dozen eggs a day from one goose! I'm looking for another goose, Sam Pig.'

Another goose! Sam Pig gasped and gazed round, also looking for another goose.

'If I can find another I shall have four dozen eggs a day, and I can give plenty away. I can give some to your family, for I don't think you get enough eggs, do you? You look very hungry, poor Sam.'

'Our hens don't lay in snowy weather,' said Sam 'I've got some eggs today, but these are the first we've had, and I am just taking them home.'

The Fox picked up the basket and looked contemptuously at the brown eggs, warm from the nest.

'You should see my eggs, Sam. Four times as big as these, and full of meat. Why, one of my eggs would make an omelette for all your family, including Badger. Yes, with Badger too! These are miserable eggs, Sam. I wouldn't give a handful of snow for eggs like these. Are they from pigeons or wrens?'

'They are hen eggs,' Sam reassured the Fox, and he peeped at the eggs lying in the basket. It was true, they were not as large as he had thought.

'Mister Fox,' said he. 'Could you – do you think you could – er – may I see some of the eggs from the snow goose? I've never seen a snow goose's eggs.'

The Fox didn't speak for a moment. He frowned as if he were making up his mind on some difficult matter.

'Well, as you are a friend of mine, Sam Pig, and as you were so kind, so very kind to me, showing me the snow goose and saving my life, I will let you have a sight of the eggs. But mind, don't tell everybody about them, or others will be going after the snow geese.'

The Fox picked up the basket of eggs and told Sam to follow him. They went into the wood, and the Fox stopped by an oak-tree.

'There they are,' he whispered. 'She's been laying astray again. That's another dozen. Goodness me! Three dozen in one day! We simply can't get through them.'

Sam saw a snowy nest under the tree, and in it a dozen great oval eggs, white as snow, gleamed in the sun.

The Fox stooped and picked one up and stroked it lovingly.

'A beautiful egg! A marvel! Cold because it was laid by my lovely snow goose, but when I put it by the fire it will get warm. This will make a good dinner for a family! How lucky I am! A nest full of new-laid eggs.'

He turned to Sam quickly. Sam was stooping over the eggs. It was amazing. They were smooth and beautiful, and white as snow. He had never imagined such big eggs, and all laid by one snow goose!

'Sam,' said the Fox softly. 'Little Sam Pig. I tell you what I will do. I will give you these eggs. Yes, I will. I will give you these eggs to take home for your brothers and Ann and Badger. Badger will be delighted. His mouth will water when he sees them! Tom will cook them and you will all have a treat.'

'Oh thank you,' cried Sam. 'Thank you, Mister Fox. It *is* kind of you.'

'Not at all,' said the Fox. 'You deserve them, Sam.' He took the hen eggs out of the basket and dropped them casually in the snow.

'You won't want these, Sam. You won't ever want to taste hen eggs when once you've had eggs from a snow goose. There's a different flavour, an aroma, in a snow goose egg. Your appetites will be whetted, yes, that's the word, whetted, when you get these eggs.'

Sam nodded and glanced disdainfully at the little brown eggs which lay rejected in the snow. The Fox was already filling the basket with the snow goose eggs. The basket was piled high with the glittering frosty ovals.

'If I were you, Sam,' advised the Fox, as Sam lifted the heavy basket, 'if I were you I should see if you can hatch one of those eggs, because a gosling might come out of it. Then you would have a goose of your own. What do you think of that?'

Sam beamed joyfully. A snow gosling! A little bird all glittering white which would soon lay two dozen eggs.

'I will, Mister Fox,' he cried. 'I love goslings.'

'So do I, Sam,' agreed the Fox. 'I see that you and I are birds of a feather, as the old saying is. Birds of a feather flock together. We must flock together, Sam.'

Sam looked shyly at the Fox, not understanding his words, but secretly flattered. He had always misjudged the Fox, and really he was a kind friend.

'Put it in your bed, Sam, and it may hatch out to-night if the bed is warm enough,' said the Fox.

So Sam went home with the basket of eggs from the snow goose, and the Fox stooped and picked up the hen eggs and filled his pockets.

'Thank you, Sam Pig,' said he softly, and he galloped away with a smile on his face.

'Where have you been, Sam?' asked Bill, as Sam came up the garden path with his heavy basket dragging his arm. 'You've been a long time gathering a few eggs.'

Sam didn't speak, but he walked into the house and put the basket on the table.

'Look!' he cried triumphantly. 'Look, all of you. Bill, Tom, Ann! Come here and look! Eggs from a snow goose. Eggs laid by a snow goose.'

The pigs picked up the eggs and turned them over and sniffed at them. 'Eggs from a snow goose? What do you mean, Sam? Where are the real eggs?'

'Oh, I threw them away. These are much better. Look at the size! One egg will be enough for all of us, Badger too.'

'Who's talking about Badger?' asked a gruff voice, and old Brock came lumbering in. 'What's that you've got, Sam?'

'A dozen eggs laid by the snow goose, Brock,' cried Sam, turning eagerly to the Badger. 'And I'm going to put one of them in my bed to hatch into a snow gosling.'

Badger picked up an egg and squeezed it in his strong paw, but it was as hard as ice.

'Eggs laid by a snow goose,' he said slowly, 'and brought home by the biggest goose of all.'

He tossed the egg in the fire, and, with a sizzle and hiss, a stream of water ran out upon the hearth.

'Snow goose! Snow gosling!' said Badger again.

Poor Sam Pig never heard the end of that. The tale ran through the woods, so that the squirrels laughed in the tree tops and the moles chuckled under the earth. Little Sam Pig had carried a basket of snow-balls home and given his hen eggs to the Fox in exchange. Snow goose! Snow goose!

The Christmas Box

It was December, and every morning when Sam Pig awoke he thought about Christmas Day. He looked at the snow, and he shivered a little as he pulled on his little trousers and ran downstairs. But the kitchen was warm and bright and a big fire burned in the hearth. Tom cooked the porridge and Ann set the table with spoons and plates, and Sam ran out to sweep the path or to find a log for the fire.

After breakfast Sam fed the birds. They came flying down from the woods, hundreds of them, fluttering and crying and stamping their tiny feet, and flapping their slender wings. The big birds – the green wood-peckers, the blue-spangled jays, the dusky rooks and the speckled thrushes – ate from large earthen dishes and stone troughs which Sam filled with scraps. They were always so hungry that the little birds got no chance, so Sam had a special breakfast table for robins and tom tits, for wrens and chaffinches. On a long flat stone were ranged rows of little polished bowls filled with crumbs and savouries. The bowls were walnut-

shells, and every bird had its own tiny brown nutshell.
Sam got the shells from the big walnut-tree in the
corner of the farmer's croft. When autumn came
the nuts fell to the ground, and Sam carried them
home in a sack. The walnuts were made into nut-

meal, but the shells were kept for the smallest birds.

After the bird-feeding Sam went out on his sledge. Sometimes Bill and Tom and Ann rode with him. Badger had made the sledge, but he never rode on it himself. He was too old and dignified, but he enjoyed watching the four pigs career down the field and roll in a heap at the bottom.

'Good old Badger,' thought Sam. 'I will give him a nice Christmas present this year. I'll make him something to take back to his house in the woods when he goes for his winter sleep.'

Badger of course never retired before Christmas, but when the festival was over he disappeared for three months and left the little family alone.

That was as far as Sam got. Ann was busy knitting a muffler for Badger. It was made of black and white sheep's wool, striped to match Badger's striped head. Bill the gardener was tending a blue hyacinth which he kept hidden in the wood-shed. Tom the cook had made a cake for Brock. It was stuffed with currants and cherries and almonds as well as many other things like honey-comb and ants' eggs. Only young Sam had nothing at all.

There was plenty of time to make a present, he told himself carelessly, and he swept up the snow from the path and collected the small birds' walnut-shells.

'Christmas is coming,' said a robin brightly. 'Have you got your Christmas cards ready, Sam?'

'Christmas cards?' said Sam. 'What's that?'

'You don't know what a Christmas card is? Why, I'm part of a Christmas card! You won't have a good Christmas without a few cards, Sam.'

Sam went back to the house where Ann sat by the fire knitting Badger's muffler. She used a pair of holly-wood knitting needles which Sam had made. A pile of scarlet holly-berries lay in a bowl by her side and she knitted a berry into the wool for ornament here and there. The blackthorn knitting needles with their little white flowers were, of course, put away for the winter. She only used those to knit spring garments.

Sam sat down by her side and took up the ball of wool. He rubbed it on his cheek and hesitated, but Ann went on knitting. She wondered what he was going to say.

'Ann. Can I make a Christmas card for Badger?' he asked.

Ann pondered this for a time, and her little needles clicked in tune with her thoughts.

'Yes, I think you can,' said she at last. 'I had forgotten what a Christmas card was like. Now I remember. There is a paintbox in the kitchen drawer, very, very old. It belonged to our grandmother. She used to collect colours from the flowers and she kept them in a box. Go and look for it, Sam.'

Sam went to the drawer and turned over the odd collection of things. There were cough-lozenges and candle-ends, and bits of string, and a bunch of rusty keys, a piece of soap and a pencil, all stuck together with gum from the larch-trees. Then, at the back of the drawer, buried under dead leaves and dried moss he found the little paintbox.

'Here it is! Oh Ann! How exciting,' cried Sam, and he carried it to the table.

'It's very dry and the paints all look the same colour,' said Ann, 'but with a good wash they'll be all right.'

'It's a very nice box of paints,' said Sam, and he licked each paint carefully with his pointed tongue.

'They taste delicious,' said he, smacking his lips. 'The colours are all different underneath, and the tastes are like the colours. Look Ann! Here's red, and here's green and here's blue, all underneath this browny colour.'

He held out the box of licked paints which were now gaily coloured.

'The red tastes of tomatoes and the green of wood-sorrel and the blue of forget-me-nots,' said Sam.

Badger was much interested in the paintbox when he came in.

'You will want a paint-brush,' said he. 'You can't use the besom-brush, or the scrubbing-brush, or even your tooth-brush to paint a Christmas card, Sam.'

'Nor can he use the Fox's brush,' teased Bill.

Badger plucked a few hairs from his tail and bound them together.

'Here! A badger-brush will be excellent, Sam.'

'What shall I have to paint on?' asked Sam, as he sucked the little brush to a point and rubbed it on one of the paints.

That puzzled everybody. There was no paper at all. They looked high and low, but it wasn't till Tom was cooking the supper that they found the right thing. Tom cracked some eggs and threw the shells in the corner. Sam took one up and used the badger-brush upon it.

'This is what I will have,' he cried, and indeed it was perfect, so smooth and delicate. Bill cut the edges neatly and Sam practised his painting upon it, making curves and flourishes.

'That isn't like a Christmas card,' said Ann, leaning over his shoulder. 'A Christmas card must have a robin on it.'

'You must ask the robin to come and be painted

tomorrow,' said Brock. 'He will know all about it. Robins have been painted on Christmas cards for many years.'

After the birds' breakfast the next day Sam asked the robin to come and have a picture made.

'I will sit here on this holly branch,' said the robin.

'Here is the snow, and here's the holly. I can hold a sprig of mistletoe in my beak if you like.'

So Sam fetched his little stool and sat in the snow with his paintbox and the badger-brush, and the robin perched on the holly branch, with a mistletoe sprig in its beak. It puffed out its scarlet breast and stared with unwinking brown eye at Sam, and he licked his brush and dipped it in the red and blue and green, giving the robin a blue feather and a green wing.

'More eggshells,' called Sam, and he painted so fast and so brightly that the robin took one look and flew away in disgust.

'That's a bird of Paradise,' said he crossly.

Sam took his eggshells indoors and hid them in a hole in the wall, ready for Christmas Day.

'Have you a Christmas present for Badger?' asked Ann. 'I have nearly finished my scarf, and Tom's cake is made, and Bill's hyacinth is in bud. What have you made, Sam?'

'Nothing except the Christmas card,' confessed Sam. 'I've been thinking and thinking, but I can't find anything. If I could knit a pair of stockings, or grow a cabbage, or make a pasty I should know what to give him, but I can't do nothing.'

'Anything,' corrected Ann.

'Nothing,' said Sam. 'I can only play my fiddle —'

'And fall in the river and steal a few apples, and get lost and catch the wind—' laughed Ann. 'Never mind. You shall share my scarf if you like, Sam, for you helped to find the sheep's wool and you got the holly berries for me.'

Sam shook his head. 'No. I won't share. I'll do something myself.'

He went out to the woods, trudging through the snow, looking for Christmas presents. In the holly-trees were scarlet clusters of berries, and the glossy ivy was adorned with black beads. The rest of the trees, except the yews and fir-trees, were bare, and they stood with boughs uplifted, and their trunks faintly smudged with snow. There wasn't a Christmas present anywhere among them. The willows, from which Badger had made the boat, were smooth and ruddy, with never a parcel or packet or treasure among them. Then something waved in a thorn bush, something fluttered like a white flag, and Sam ran forward. The wind was rising and it made a curious moan and a whistle as it ruffled Sam's ears and made them ache. He stretched up to the little flag and found it was a feather. A feather! Sam had a thought! Perhaps the wind blew it to him, but there it was, a feather!

'I'll make him a feather bed, and when he goes to

his castle deep in the woods he will take it with him to lie on. Poor old Badger, sleeping alone on the hard ground. Yes, I'll make him a feather bed.'

When the birds came for their breakfast the next morning Sam spoke to them about it.

'Can you spare a feather or two? I want to make a feather bed for old Badger's Christmas present,' he told them.

The birds shook their wings and dropped each a loose feather; they brushed and combed themselves and tossed little feathers to the ground. They passed the word round among the tree families, and other birds came flying with little feathers in their beaks for Sam Pig. A flock of starlings left a heap of glistening shot-silk, and the rooks came cawing from the bare elms with sleek black quills. The chattering magpies brought their black and white feathers, which Sam thought were like Badger's head. The jays came with their bright blue jewels, and the robins with scarlet wisps from their breasts. A crowd of tits gave him their own soft little many-coloured feathers, and even the wood pigeons left grey feathers for Sam. He had so many the air was clouded with feathers so that it seemed to be snowing again.

He gathered them up and filled his sack, and even then he had some over. He put the beautiful tiny feathers in his pocket, the red scraps from the robins, the blue petals of feathers from the tits, the yellow atoms from the goldfinches and the emerald-blue gems from the kingfisher. These he wove into a basket as small as a nutshell, for Sister Ann, and inside he put some mistletoe pearls. Ann would like this, he knew.

On Christmas Day Sam came downstairs to the kitchen, calling 'A merry Christmas' to everybody. He didn't hang up his stocking of course because he had no stockings, and he didn't expect any presents either. Badger was the one who got the presents, old Badger who was the friend and guardian of the four pigs. It was at Christmas time they made their gifts to thank him for his care. So all the little pigs came hurrying downstairs with their presents for him.

There stood Badger, waiting for them, with a twinkle in his eye. Ann gave him the black and white muffler with its little scarlet berries interwoven.

'Here's a muffler for cold days in the forest, Brock,' said she.

'Just the thing for nights when I go hunting,' said Brock, nodding his head and wrapping the muffler round his neck.

Then Bill gave him the little blue hyacinth growing in a pot.

With luv - BiLL

To deer BROCK From TOM

'Here's a flower for you, Brock, which I've reared myself.'

'Thank you, Bill. It's the flower I love,' said Brock and he sniffed the sweet scent.

Then Tom came forward with the cake, which was prickly with almonds and seeds from many a plant.

'Here's a cake, Brock, and it has got so many things inside it, I've lost count of them, but there's honey-comb and eggs.'

'Ah! You know how I like a slice of cake,' cried Brock, taking the great round cake which was heavy as lead.

Then little Sam came, with the feather bed on his back. He had embroidered it with the letter B made of the black and white magpie feathers.

'For you to sleep on in your castle,' said he.

'Sam! Sam!' everybody cried. 'And you kept it secret! That's what you were doing every morning when the birds came for their breakfast! We thought there seemed to be a lot of feathers on the ground!'

Badger lay down on the little bed and pretended to snore. He was delighted with the warm comfortable present from little Sam Pig.

'Never mind the weather but sleep upon a feather,' said he. 'I shall sleep like a top through the fiercest gale when I lie on this little bed.'

They had breakfast, with a lashing of treacle on their porridge from the tin which Ann had kept for festivals. Then Sam hurried out to feed the birds and to thank them again for their share in Badger's Christmas. He carried a basket full of walnut-shells stuffed with scraps, and he found hosts of birds hopping about waiting for him.

But when he stepped into the garden he gave a cry of surprise, for in the flower bed grew a strange little tree.

'Look! Look!' he called. 'Ann! Bill! Tom! Badger! Come and look! It wasn't growing there last night. Where has it come from? And look at the funny fruit hanging on it! What is it?'

They followed him out and stared in astonishment at the small fir-tree, all hung with pretty things. There were sugar pigs with pink noses and curly tails of string; and sugar watches with linked chains of white sugar, and chocolate mice. There were rosy apples and golden oranges, and among the sweet dainties were glittering icicles and hoar-frost crystals.

'Where has it come from? How did it grow here?' they asked, and they turned to Badger. 'Is it a magic?' they asked. 'Will it disappear? Is it really real?'

'It's solid enough, for the tree has come from the

woods, but the other things will disappear fast enough I warrant when you four get near them.'

'But where did you find such strange and lovely things?' persisted Ann, staring up with her little blue eyes. 'Where? Where? From fairyland, Badger?'

'I went to the Christmas fair in the town. I walked up to a market stall and bought them with a silver penny I had by me,' said Brock.

'But did nobody say anything to you?' asked Sam. 'How did you escape?'

'They were all so busy they didn't notice a little brown man who walked among them. They didn't bother about me on Christmas Eve. Miracles happen on Christmas Eve, and perhaps I was one of them. Also I carried the Leprechaun's shoe in my hand and maybe that helped me.'

Then Sam Pig brought the little feather basket and hung it among the icicles for his sister Ann. She was enchanted by it, and strung the mistletoe pearls round her neck.

'But where are your Christmas cards, Sam?' she asked suddenly. 'This is the time to give them.'

'I sat on them, Ann,' confessed Sam. 'I put them on a chair and sat down on them.'

'Crushed Christmas cards,' murmured Tom the cook. 'They will do very well to give an extra flavour to the soup. Those reds and blues and greens will make the soup taste extra good I'm sure.'

It was true. The Christmas soup with the Christmas card flavour was the nicest anyone had ever tasted, and not a drop was left.

As for the Christmas tree, everybody shared it, for the birds flew down to its branches and sang a Christmas carol in thanks for their breakfasts, and Sam sat underneath and sang another carol in thanks for their feathers.

So it was a very happy Christmas all round.